IT'S ALL FUN AND GAMES

IT'S ALL FUN AND GAMES

DAVE BARRETT

This is a work of fiction. Names, characters, organizations, places, events, and incidents are either products of the author's imagination or are used fictitiously.

Published by Inkshares, Inc., San Francisco, California, as part of the Nerdist Collection
www.inkshares.com

Edited and designed by Girl Friday Productions
www.girlfridayproductions.com

Cover design by Elsie Lyons
Cover images via Shutterstock: © Vaclav Hroch; © Sergey Kamshylin; © Iakov Filimonov; © Igorsky; © Sensay; © Alex Bond; © faestock; © Dmitriy Karelin.

ISBN: 9781941758816
e-ISBN: 9781941758823

Library of Congress Control Number: 2015955890

First edition

Printed in the United States of America.

To Lloyd Alexander, whose Chronicles of Prydain *taught me that worlds of magic and adventure exist; and to Gary Gygax, who taught me how to play in them.*

And to my brother, Jim, my first Dungeon Master.

PROLOGUE

"Run! *Now!*" TJ shouted, yanking Allison's sleeve. Her eyes were focused on the ground, where their friend lay twitching slightly. An arrow shaft stuck out of his chest. Her first thought was that it was all part of the game—just some elaborate prank for the newbies on their first outing. If so, it wasn't very funny.

But there was no way that arrow was fake. The noise it had made when it struck. The blood that was rapidly spreading across his clothes. The raspy way he was breathing and the saliva slowly trickling from between his lips. Allison felt another yank on her shoulder as TJ shouted, "Leave him for now!" She shrugged off his grasp, reaching down to try to drag her injured friend by the collar. After a few moments she gave up the effort.

A sudden force struck her in the shoulder and spun her around. Dazed, she looked for whoever had hit her and saw no one standing nearby. Instead, she found a second arrow stuck in the wall, still quivering with spent energy. She reached up to her shoulder and felt a dent in the metal of her breastplate. A quick look back revealed that the archer in the woods had drawn a third arrow and was fitting it to his bow, a determined look on his face. With a cry of anguish and one last glance at her fallen friend, she turned and fled after TJ and the others.

CHAPTER 1

The bell rang, cutting their teacher off midsentence, and the students began stuffing books and papers into their backpacks. There was a sense of urgency in their movements, as if somehow the clock might change its mind if they dallied.

"We'll pick up from where we left off on Tuesday," Mr. Simmons called out over the noise. "Everyone please read pages two hundred forty to two hundred fifty-six in the text, and have a nice long weekend. Don't work too hard!" The last he said with a smile, knowing that the likelihood of anyone actually reading pages two hundred forty to two hundred fifty-six were just this side of zero. Besides, not working too hard was advice he planned on taking—he was headed into the backwoods to go fishing.

"So are you going to come, or no?" TJ Keller flashed his lopsided grin at his best friend, Allison Duggan. "You know you want to." He added in a singsong voice, "You know it will be fuuunnn!"

Allison, a scrawny strawberry-blonde girl, tried to not smile back, but failed. "No, I really don't want to. In fact, I don't think I can possibly explain to you just how little I want to. I don't care what you say. Getting all dressed up like wizards and sleeping out in the woods doesn't seem even remotely like a fun thing to do." Despite the smirk, TJ could tell she was serious.

"Aww, come on," he pouted. "First of all, not everyone gets dressed up like a wizard. That's only me. A party of wizards would never survive very long. You need some tanks to melee, and a healer, and if possible a rogue to pick locks and disarm traps and stuff. Otherwise, we end up having the barbarian just triggering all the traps we find and he soaks up all the damage. That's hardly an elegant solution." He looked ready to continue, but Allison raised her eyebrows. "Yeah well, anyway, other people have different costumes." He paused, then added with a sly look, "And Simon is coming!"

"Whoa. Simon? As in Simon Williams? Really? What would he be doing at one of your geek fests? Doesn't he have a football game this weekend?" Simon was the starting halfback for the school's team. As a sophomore, he should have been sitting on the bench, but an injury to the star senior promoted him to starter a year early. He was tall and handsome, and all of the underclass girls—and most of the upper class as well—harbored secret crushes on him. Allison was no exception, and TJ knew it.

TJ shouldered his backpack and swiped a few stray eraser shavings off the top of his desk. He flourished an "after you" motion with his arm and followed behind as Allison headed toward the door. "Team is off this week because of the long weekend. Plus, they want to give students the ability to rest and recharge a bit before No Child Left Behind tests start up next week." No one—including the teachers and administrators—looked forward to the week of standardized tests that occurred three times a year. Freeport Central High School wasn't a failing school by any stretch of the imagination, but it wasn't one of western Massachusetts's star performers either. "I guess they figured we could use all the help we can get. Maybe they think it will prevent a few concussions and that will help keep scores up."

Allison snickered as they walked to the hallway with their lockers. "But I mean, what's he doing hanging out in the woods doing all that magic stuff? No offense, but that hardly seems very football playery."

TJ heaved an exaggerated sigh as he spun the combination on his locker and opened it up. Inside were several pieces of artwork from last year's Tolkien calendar and a little figurine of a dragon with a ruby crystal in its mouth. "First of all, have you ever noticed that when someone says 'no offense,' they're about to say something really offensive? Just saying." Allison chuckled again and punched him in the shoulder. "Anyway," he continued, "some people had lives before high school. It just so happens that before he got all tall and handsome and buff and athletic, he was something of a geek too. His big brother came home from school with a *Dungeons and Dragons* rulebook one day and he was hooked. I've seen him at some gaming events from time to time over the years, but since freshman year, when he started playing football in the fall and running track in the spring, he's kinda dropped out of the scene."

"So why is he getting back into it now?"

"You got me. I just saw his name on the list of people who signed up for this weekend's event. From what I understand, the story line is going to be pretty epic. Maybe it was just too good for him to pass up. If you come, you'll be able to ask him yourself."

"Yeah, I don't know. Who else is coming?" TJ could see Allison was beginning to waver. As they walked down the hallway to where her own locker was, he began ticking off names.

"Well, there's Jimmy, of course. He's been talking about it for weeks, even replaced most of his equipment and added a few pieces of armor. I bet he's going to look pretty slick."

Allison's eyebrow was cocked again, and he shot her a wry grin.

"Yeah, well, take my word for it," TJ continued. "He's big into the details, no joke. So yeah, there's Jimmy. Chuckles will hopefully make an appearance, though he hasn't confirmed yet. If we end up in any dungeons this weekend and don't have a thief handy, we're going to be in some deep trouble." He grinned at his pun, and Allison rolled her eyes. TJ shrugged. "Well, they can't all be winners. Oh, there's this guy Stu, whom I haven't met, but Jimmy says he's pretty cool. His mom can sew really well, and she made him this full costume in forest greens and browns, so he's all camoed and stuff. I think that's it."

Allison stopped in front of her locker and began working the combination. "So what you're saying is that I'm going to be the only girl?"

"Well, Leslie Tiller is going to be there. She's really nice, but not your type." Leslie also played for the football team. As starting nose tackle. TJ gestured to the inside of Allison's locker. Hanging inside were her first pair of pointe shoes and a photo of herself posing with a counselor at the performing arts camp where she spent much of her summers.

"Gotcha. Well, fair enough."

"And those are really the only people *I* know are coming. There are always lots of other folks who show up whom I've never met before. People from other areas who travel about. Newbies coming for the first time. There aren't going to be many, but are you going to be the only girl there?" He shrugged.

"I doubt it. And anyway, look at it this way. That's fewer girls around Simon this weekend. Maybe you guys could really hit it off."

"Yeah, right." She didn't sound convinced.

TJ shot her his best smile. "Mayyybeee . . ."

Allison gave him a long-suffering look and sighed as she shut her locker. "Oh, OK. I'll come, though if it's not fun, I'm blaming you. K? And you have to come to Bring a Friend Day at the dance studio this spring. In a tutu."

The grin on his face faltered slightly as images of ballet flashed through his mind, but he recovered quickly. "K! What are best friends for?" They turned from the lockers and headed outside to the buses. "My gear is all packed already. I'll come home with you and help you get your stuff together. You wouldn't happen to have a bedroll, would you?" The incredulous look on her face answered the question. "Though I guess a regular sleeping bag will do the trick," he blurted. As TJ rattled on about the advantages of wool fabric versus cotton for cloaks, Allison wondered if she knew what she was getting herself into.

CHAPTER 2

The air was crisp the next morning when TJ's mom pulled into Allison's driveway. The weather forecast predicted a beautiful weekend: clear skies, highs in the lower seventies, and lows only in the upper fifties. Nothing a bedroll—or a sleeping bag—couldn't handle. Despite the warm temperatures, autumn was in the air and the leaves had begun to change color. As far as TJ could tell, it all pointed to a glorious event. He hopped out of the car and went to ring the doorbell. He waited a few moments and then rang the bell again.

"Geez, keep your shirt on, I'll be right there!" Allison's voice was muffled through the heavy door. Sighing, TJ leaned back against the low railing that surrounded the porch and prepared to wait. Allison's parents, having learned of her last-minute plans to go "fight monsters" in the surrounding countryside, wasted no time planning their own weekend getaway. They were flying out to Atlantic City for two nights at one of the newest and ugliest casinos on the boardwalk. Their cab had come to take them away at 5:00 a.m., and they were no doubt already in the air toward their glitzy weekend. Allison was an only child, so there wasn't anyone else to invite TJ in. He sighed again.

Suddenly, the door jerked open. TJ's jaw dropped at the sight of Allison's costume. There she was—at least he thought it was her—dressed ready for a battle, an opera, or maybe both. She had donned a sky-blue dress that swirled around her legs in the light breeze caused by the opening door. Her torso was encased in a plastic replica of a bronze breastplate, with outrageously sized domes on her chest. Topping off the ensemble was a Viking helmet, one giant horn turned up and one turned down.

"So, how do I look? Am I going to fit in?" Allison grinned from ear to ear.

"Um. Well. Um." TJ stalled as he tried to formulate a response. "That's not exactly what we discussed on your packing list last night. What happened?"

"Well, you know how my uncle has that amateur theater company over on Jefferson Street? I gave him a call last night and this is what he dropped off. I think I look smashing!" She gave a little twirl, letting the bottom of the robes billow out into a bell shape around her legs. "He said that I need to make sure that I don't get it dirty, but I'm sure these robes can be dry-cleaned if it comes to that."

"Well. Um."

Allison's eyes narrowed and she gave her friend a little pout. "You're not going to tell me I look ridiculous, are you? Because if so, you're off to slay dragons this weekend alone." She nodded curtly for emphasis.

TJ needed only the slightest pause to blurt out, "Oh no, Allie! You've got that look down. I think you're going to fit right in!" In truth, he was pretty sure that she wouldn't. But he knew that geeks are notoriously unwilling to mock the way other people dress, so she wouldn't actually hear anything about it. He just hoped no one was planning on bringing a camera. The last thing he wanted was to cause ridicule for his best friend for the rest of her life.

"By the way," she added suspiciously. "Why aren't you dressed yet? This isn't some big joke, is it?"

"Oh no," he replied hurriedly. "I just have the wizard robe and hat. I'll toss them on when we get there."

She looked appeased, but he still decided a strategic change of subject was in order. "Where's all your stuff? Let me help you get it loaded up."

"Oh, I don't have a whole lot of stuff to bring. There's my sleeping bag. I mean bedroll." She flashed a grin. "And I've got just a few other things. It all fits in my backpack over there. If you want to grab it, I'll get my bedroll and we can hit the road." TJ stepped inside the house. Her bag was waiting beneath a small cherry table. The lights from the chandelier overhead reflected in the mirror that faced the door. For perhaps the millionth time, he considered how cool it must be to have two lawyers for parents. The backpack looked just as advertised, but when he hefted it onto his shoulder he let out a groan.

"Good grief, what have you got in this thing? Rocks?"

Allison turned, then snorted a laugh and replied, "Yeah, actually. Those are rocks my folks and I collected last weekend when we went hiking. You know how they are. Dad read a book about family bonding, and they decided it would be a good experience to go play geologist. My weekend bag is that one." She pointed to another backpack sitting by the door.

TJ shrugged and trudged over to an identical backpack, then threw it easily over his shoulder and headed out the door. Allison followed him through, her sleeping bag in hand.

Checking that her keys were in her pocket, she pulled the door shut, twisted the knob to make sure that it was locked, and then skipped down the walkway to where TJ waited at the open trunk. She tossed the bag into the trunk and twirled over to the passenger-side back door.

TJ let out a chuckle and said in a surprised voice, "Well now, that's quite the turnaround, isn't it? I pretty much had to twist your arm to come yesterday, and now you're raring to go!"

"Well, I decided that if I'm going to look like an idiot for a couple days, I may as well have fun doing it. And if it stinks, I can always grab a ride with someone back home and then spend all day tomorrow eating Cap'n Crunch in my pj's and binge watching Cartoon Network in an otherwise empty house. Win-win, if you ask me!"

TJ barked a laugh and shook his head. "That's the spirit! I knew I liked you for a reason, Allie."

She hopped into the passenger-side backseat and said, "Hi, Mrs. Keller. Thanks for the ride!"

"My pleasure, Allie," his mom replied cheerfully. "It's great to see you! Hopefully, we'll get you over for dinner again soon."

TJ went around to the rear door on the driver side and got in. As he buckled in, he said, "I'm not going to leave you back here all by yourself, you know."

She grinned and buckled her own belt.

The car pulled out of the driveway and moved slowly down the street. Allison looked back at her house before turning her attention to her friend, who had begun to talk about his character's past exploits. The well-manicured lawn and perfect little hedges seemed to mock her decision to spend the weekend with their wilder cousins—poison ivy, poison sumac, and poison who-knows-what-else. But one thing was sure: TJ really seemed to have fun on these things, so maybe it wouldn't be so bad after all.

The trip took less than thirty minutes on the highway. The group TJ played with had booked a wildlife reserve for the weekend. It was the type of place that Boy Scout troops use for campouts—a good mixture of open land and woods, as well as a few small ponds scattered here and there. Most important, there was a central lodge with running water and even an outdoor shower. On those rainy weekends when people ended the day all covered in mud, even a cold shower was better than nothing, especially when there was a large open hearth waiting to warm them up.

The property's owner had originally been wary of letting a bunch of teens and young adults run around pretending to chop each other into pieces, and so he had stayed on-site for the first game. It turned out that he had so much fun he decided to keep coming back and was eventually given the role of King of the Realm. Everyone understood that if they didn't treat the property with respect, not only would the group have to find a new place, but it was entirely possible their character would lose their head to the executioner's axe.

After the friends pulled their bags out of the trunk, TJ reached back in and removed his costume. He pulled the ornate robe over his head and then topped himself with a floppy hat. "The beauty of robes is that no one knows what you're wearing underneath. A couple layers of sweats go a long way on chilly evenings. Some folks go for period shoes as well, but if I have to run, I'd rather it be in my Nikes than a pair of sandals."

After the requisite hug and admonition to be safe from TJ's mother, the two friends were left standing in a gravel lot adjacent to the lodge, backpacks slung across their shoulders.

"So now what?" Allison asked.

“Now we go get ourselves checked in, see who else is here, and get you a character!”

The pair walked the short distance to the building and slipped through the open door. The room was dark, as one might expect of some medieval tavern. Unfortunately, also like a tavern, the room smelled of unwashed bodies. Sitting in chairs around the room were a couple dozen teenagers in various layers of fantasy gear, each individual’s choice apparently based on their individual physique. Simon, the football player, was something of an outlier, so Allison saw a lot of flowing robes, but no gladiator-style leather harnesses.

Allison had to choke down a laugh at the assembled players, and TJ elbowed her in the ribs. “Shh,” he whispered at her. “They have ears too, so be kind. They’re really nice folks, I promise. Let’s go get us registered.”

In one corner of the room was a desk with official-looking people and a sign that read “Ye Olde Registration” behind it. As they headed in that direction they heard, “Hey, TJ! You made it! And you brought a newbie! Awesome!” The voice came from the opposite corner of the room. The two turned, and TJ broke into a wide grin as he spotted some of his friends gathered around a small table. He took Allison’s elbow and guided her over.

“Hey, guys! Great to see you again. Is this going to be a great weekend, or what?” This was met with vigorous nodding. “And look who I finally managed to convince! You remember my friend Allison, don’t you? Through sheer determination and the promise of hot guys, I convinced her to give in and join us for the weekend.”

The assembled boys looked back and forth at each other in amusement. One said, “Hot guys, huh? I didn’t know I was your type, TJ.” He batted his eyelashes, and the others at the table laughed. "And of course we remember Allison," he added with a snort. "It's not like you ever shut up about her or anything."

TJ's face turned red. "Come *on*, Chuck. You look in a mirror lately? I told her Simon was coming, and that's what pushed her over the edge." Heads nodded in understanding. "Anyway, Allison, this is the party. Chuck, our thief extraordinaire, can open just about any lock that exists. And we haven't found a trap yet he couldn't disarm."

The small, slightly chubby boy was dressed all in black, with the exception of a conspicuously thick silver chain dangling from his neck. He smiled proudly and declared, "I've put all my points into those two skills. I'm totally worthless for pretty much everything else, but I can break us into places that no one else's character will ever see. I'm up to eight points in each, TJ. I leveled up last game. Gained a bonus weapon skill too, so now I can actually swing a dagger without hitting one of you guys."

A large boy sitting next to him said, "That's what you think. I'm still keeping my distance from you, little guy." He stood up and extended a meaty hand. At his full height he towered over everyone else at the table, and Allison had to look up to meet his eye. "Hey, Allison, good to see you again. It's been too long."

She took his hand and shook it a few times. "Nice to see you too, Jimmy. You got big over the summer, didn't you?"

Chuck piped in. "And once again, Ford Prefect's assessment of humanity's ability to cheerfully state the obvious proves true!" Allison looked at him blankly. "C'mon. Ford Prefect? *Hitchhiker's Guide to the Galaxy*?" She blinked. He glanced at TJ. "Where did you find her? Man, she needs some serious edumacation. Learn you a book."

Allison flashed Chuck a hostile look.

TJ shrugged and gave her a quick shoulder hug. "She's a work in progress."

Not only had Jimmy grown, but TJ's prediction about his outfit was correct. He had a shimmering coat of mail over a padded gambeson, metal bracers attached to his forearms, and what looked like matching pieces strapped to his legs. "Nice getup you've got there," Allison said, nodding at his costume in approval.

"Thanks," he replied, and gave her a mock curtsy. "You know how my mom is. Once she got it into her head that I needed to look beefy, she went all out." Allison nodded in agreement. His dad had died when Jimmy was in kindergarten, and ever since then, his mom tended to overcompensate. He always had the best of everything, even when she had to stretch.

The third member at the table, a boy with light-brown skin and bony shoulders, stood up and extended a hand to TJ. He was clothed head to toe in shades of green, with a tunic, cloak, leggings, and blouse. Large ears poked out of his brown polar-fleece slouch hat. Leaning against the wall behind him was a bow, whose style Allison recognized from their archery unit in PE class. The bow had a wood-grain texture. Next to it rested a full quiver, whose arrows had been inserted with their fletching downward. Cushioned, rounded tips poked out from the quiver's mouth.

"You're Stu, aren't you? I'm TJ. Pleased to meet you."

Stu nodded. "Likewise. I've heard good things about you from Jimmy at school, and I'm eager to fight by your side." He turned to Allison and took her hand. Rather than shaking it, he bowed, brushing his lips across the back of it. "Milady."

Allison giggled and said, "Well, I can't say anyone's ever done that before. Maybe this weekend won't be a total bust!" The boys laughed. "Hi, Stuart! What are you doing out here at this geek fest?"

"I needed to get out of the house for a little peace and quiet," he replied. "By the way, call me Stu. Only my mom and my sisters call me Stuart, and I kinda hate it."

"Got it!"

Chuck's brow wrinkled in confusion. "You guys know each other?"

"Now who's stating the obvious?" Allison rolled her eyes and Chuck stuck his tongue out. "Stu's two older sisters dance with me at the studio in Springfield. They're really good, though I don't think either wants to be a dancer after college or anything."

"Nope, premed for both," Stu confirmed. "Just like Dad."

"So what kinda character are you going to play, Allison?" Jimmy asked.

"Um. I don't know, actually. I didn't really give it any thought. I just figured I'd show up and hit things on the head or cast magical spells"—she wiggled her fingers—"or something along those lines. I don't even know any of the rules."

The boys at the table all looked back and forth at each other, then in unison declared, "Healer!"

"Healer? You mean I don't get to bonk people or cast magic spells or anything like that?" She shot a hurt look at TJ. "This is going to stink, isn't it?"

"No! No, it won't," TJ replied, perhaps a little too quickly. But she wasn't buying it. He continued. "Well. Maybe it will a little." TJ held up his thumb and forefinger. "But just because you're a healer, it doesn't mean you can't bonk people. We'll make sure we get you a club or a mace or something. And technically, healing is a magic spell. It's just a *different* sort of magic spell from what I cast." Allison looked unconvinced. "And, the guys are right. We've got a thief, Chuckles. We've got a wizard, me. We've got a big piece of meat, Jimmy. It looks like Stu provides us with ranged attacks and, if I'm guessing correctly, tracking and other outdoor skills that could come in handy, depending on what the story is." Stu nodded and TJ continued. "What we're really missing is healing support. There have been some adventures when we've barely been scratched and all we needed was Chuck's expertise to get us through. But if we get into some big combat and start taking damage, we're gonna be in rough shape without a healer."

"And you're already dressed as one! Sorta. Except for the hat." Jimmy's comment elicited laughs from the guys and turned Allison's face red.

"Yeah, well, you better make sure you don't get clobbered too much, 'cause I'm not sure if I *or* my hat want to heal you very much." She let out a little humpf.

This resulted in a series of "ooohs," but Jimmy just grinned. "I'll do my best. I'm good at not getting hit!"

TJ pulled on Allison's sleeve. "C'mon, let's get registered and get your character created. It won't take long, and I'll explain the rules while we're in line. Be back in a jiffy, guys."

The two left the table with a wave and crossed the room to the registration desk, where there were only a few people in line ahead of them. As they approached the line, Allison gave TJ a sideways glance. "So it's not like you ever shut up about me?"

TJ blushed a deep red, which she pretended not to notice. "Yeah . . . w-well," he stammered, then abruptly changed the subject. "Here's the way things work. The weapons we use are all made out of PVC pipe wrapped up in foam and duct-taped like crazy. It isn't comfortable to get hit by one, but it's not going to do any serious harm. Different weapons do different amounts of damage, and everyone can take only so much damage before they get knocked out. Different classes can absorb different amounts, and as you level up, your hit points increase too. You'll be starting at first level, so you aren't able to get hit much, even with your, um, armor." He tried, and failed, not to look at her absurdly large breastplate. "You should try to avoid it as much as possible."

She crossed her arms. "You think?"

"Shush, I'm trying to be helpful and put this in context for you. I've been around for a while, so even though I'm only a wizard—and we get the fewest hit points of the bunch—I'm still going to have more than you. And Jimmy, he's a beast. He could take enough damage to kill you and me both twice over and it still wouldn't put much of a crimp in his style. He's great to have around."

"Well, what keeps the monsters from just running past him and whacking us dead first?"

"Two things. First, he doesn't carry a sword. He carries a *sword*. It doesn't really fit in rooms with low ceilings. So it's hard for things to run around him, simply as a matter of logistics. Second, his class is called a berserker, and one of its traits is that enemies are drawn to fight him. In rules terms, what it means is that he wears a bright-yellow headband when we are out playing, and monsters will always attack him first, unless they physically can't get to him or someone else injures them for more than half of their total hit points. So we mostly let him go to work and support him with our other abilities from afar. Stu will be an interesting addition to the mix—we've never played with an archer. Hopefully, he's got good aim, or he'll be tagging Jimmy in the back with his arrows, and friendly fire counts too.

"As far as spellcasting goes, well, I have a list of spells that I'm allowed to cast during the day. A couple of my more powerful ones I'm only allowed once or twice. A couple of my basic spells I can cast as often as I want. I've got these little beanbags I carry in a pouch on my waist. When I want to cast a spell at someone, I call out the name of my spell and throw it at my target. If I hit, it does damage. If I miss, well, I miss. And 'cause of safety concerns, if I hit someone in the head, I take damage myself as a penalty. So good aim is important."

"Well, what about me? What will I be able to do?" They were almost to the front of the line.

"As a healer, most of your abilities will be focused on, well, healing. And as a level one, you're not going to have a lot. Nothing offensive that you could cast is going to be of any use against the things we're gonna be fighting, so we'll make sure you focus on simply keeping the rest of us alive. You know, like how you used to sit tight on defense back in soccer? And if it comes down to it, like I said, we can get you a mace to whack things with if they get too close. Again, no shots to the head or the, um, unmentionables. Those are no-no's."

At the table there was the typical paperwork: Name and emergency contacts. Known food or medicine allergies. Waiver of liability. As they filled out the forms, the man behind the registration desk asked, "Character names?"

"Galphalon," replied TJ. "And a newbie."

"Galphalon?" Allison repeated. "Where did you come up with that?"

TJ shrugged. "Dunno. Just sorta came to me. Like ten years ago. And I've stuck with it. Don't be a hater."

The administrator pulled up TJ's file and was filling out a card of abilities and spells that TJ had access to for the weekend.

"I need to have proof that Galphalon can do all the things I say he can when we get out there and start playing," TJ said in response to Allison's unasked question. "If one of the judges has any doubt, I can just show them the card and we're good to go. Saves a lot of time and confusion."

She nodded her understanding.

The administrator finished the last card with a flourish. "Here you go. What is your friend playing? And does she know the rules?" He looked her costume up and down and seemed to come to the conclusion that no, she probably didn't.

"She's going to be healing for us this weekend, and yeah, I've explained the most important parts to her."

"Healing. Good call. I've heard that the kobolds are down from the hills in force. Fighting will be fierce indeed." He pulled out a fresh character sheet. "OK, a level one healer gets access to light heal, cure poison, stun, and holy smite. You get five casts a day, to be spread among those four spells. Which do you want to load up on?"

"She'll take four heals and a cure poison. And give her a point in diplomacy, a point in maces, and a heavy armor proficiency."

The man nodded and began filling out the character card.

"Wait," Allison interrupted. "What's that holy smite thing? That sounds really . . . smiteful."

TJ shook his head. "It only does two points of damage with a successful hit. Trust me. We've got no shortage of damage-dealing ability between Jimmy, Stu, and yours truly. Those two points aren't going to be a whole lot of good for anything. What we need is healing, 'cause each of those spells gives us back five health points. She'll take the four heals and the cure poison."

She raised her voice. "Wait a minute. You asked me to come and play because it would be fun. And part of the fun is killing things and waggling my fingers and stuff. I want to be able to smite things. Just once. So I can say I did."

The registration guy gave him a sympathetic look.

TJ let out a sigh. "OK. Give her a smite. Who knows, maybe it will come in handy after all. But if I drop dead because you ran out of heals, I'm not going to be very happy with you. You hear?"

Allison gave him her best innocent look and batted her eyelashes. "Okeydokes, you're the boss!"

They got the rest of the paperwork taken care of and Allison was handed a small metal carabiner with the tokens representing her skills and spells attached to it. The pair then headed back to the corner table. A new person had arrived. The boy's face was green and covered in warts, and his hair was pure white. Completing the makeup was a pair of little horn nubs sticking out of his forehead.

"Oh hey," TJ said. "Simon's here!"

"Hi, Allison," the whatever-it-was said, grinning as he stood.

Allison's jaw dropped.

CHAPTER 3

Allison stood there, mouth agape, for what was certainly a socially awkward time. Finally, she was able to stammer, "W-whoaaaah."

"Yeah, pretty cool, isn't it?" TJ's eyes gleamed mischievously. "I didn't want to spoil the surprise for you, and I wasn't sure if he'd come all made up anyway." Allison glared, and his smile faltered. "Erm, be right back, guys. Gotta go pee."

The rest of the group seemed just as amused by the revelation. "Sorta changes the weekend of hot guys, huh?" Chuck seemed amused beyond measure, and Allison's look did nothing to suppress his mirth.

Simon looked back and forth between the two for a few moments before shrugging and returning to his seat. He patted the folding chair next to him. "Take a load off, Allie. We've got a little time to kill." Reluctantly, Allison took the offered seat, with disbelief still registered on her face. "So you're wondering why I'm here, dressed like an idiot, aren't you?"

Color spread across her cheeks, and she mumbled, "You're the one who used the *i*-word, not me."

He smiled back. "Before we all ended up on that rec soccer team my dad coached, I was totally part of the *D and D* crew with Jimmy. But then my dad decided I'd be better at peewee football. That ended up taking a lot of my time, so I had to give up the gaming. Every so often I got in a free weekend to get dressed up and fight, but my gaming days are pretty much behind me now. This is my first chance to actually play in just about forever. I'm worried it may be my last."

"Well, if this is to be your end, at least make it an end worthy of remembrance! At least, that's what Théoden said in *The Two Towers*." Jimmy grinned and raised a mock toast.

"Hear! Hear!" the others shouted, raising their own invisible glasses.

Simon smiled back at the group. "Thanks, guys. Anyway, I was a lot better at doing the makeup years ago. But if you don't use your skills, you lose your skills, right? That's what Dad always says." He paused, lost in thought, before continuing. "What are *you* doing here? I never expected you to do this in a million years!"

"Well, you know, TJ finally roped me into it. I wasn't doing anything else this weekend, so I figured I'd give it a shot."

"You got a backstory?" Chuck interjected. "Or even a name?"

Allison looked back and forth between the boys. "Backstory?"

"Well, for example, my name is Phineas! I'm the best pickpocket and cat burglar in Westmarch. Or at least I *was*, until I crossed the wrong folks in the guild and had to hop a boat outta town. Met up with these fine gentlemen and offered them my services." He jerked a thumb at Jimmy. "Always pays to have your own muscle, you know what I mean?"

Jimmy nodded. "I am Jameson MacCordish, from the northern tribes." He grinned sheepishly. "I know, it's kinda cliché, but it seemed cool when I was ten. Anyway, my village was destroyed by outlanders, and I left, seeking vengeance. Found it too. But that didn't bring my family back to life, so I've been wandering ever since."

Allison shook her head. "Well, I didn't think of any of that. No name, and definitely no backstory. Is that going to be a problem?"

"Nah," replied Jimmy. "Allison is as good a name as any, and with that hair of yours, maybe you're from the North as well." He screwed up his eyes. "In fact, let's say you're my best friend's kid sister. The two of you were away from the village when it was sacked—I bet he was taking you to the temple to start as a novice. And the last time I saw him he asked me to look after you, so here you are. Fresh from the temple and out on your first adventure!"

Allison looked doubtful, but she gave in at the happy look on Jimmy's face. "Kid sister. First adventure. Got it."

"Oye! Oye!" A herald's voice drifted in through a cracked window. "The king commands your attendance on the parade ground!" All conversation inside the lodge stopped, and bodies began moving toward the door.

TJ stuck his head in the room and called, "C'mon, guys, time to start!"

They stepped out into the bright sunlight to see that a tent had been erected. Allison figured it was probably meant to be a pavilion, since it had a couple streamers waving from its corners and apex, but the "J&R Party Rental" stamped in big letters sort of killed the effect.

She looked around at the thirty or so others who had converged for the weekend of gaming. As Allison had feared, there were almost no other girls present, though it occurred to her that she didn't feel as out of place as she'd expected. The one adult woman in attendance stood nearby and was dressed in a green outfit similar to Stu's. Next to her was a bearded man in a matching costume, and as the two murmured back and forth, they watched the play fighting of three children who looked to be between ages ten and fifteen. Occasionally one of the adults would call out a suggestion to the kids, and when the youngest took a sword in the face and burst into tears, the woman wrapped him in a hug. Realizing it was a family who had come together for the weekend, Allison smirked, idly imagining what half-human, half-whatever-Simon-was children would look like.

There were several other nonhumans within the group, though none of them appeared to have put the attention to detail into their makeup as Simon had. Those players who weren't robed mostly wore shirts woven from gray or silver yarn to simulate armor, and a couple even had headpieces made from real chain links. Almost everyone had a weapon of some sort, either a staff or a sword or an axe, all padded and duct-taped for safety.

As the last person exited the lodge, someone nearby blew a trumpet fanfare and then shouted, "Hail King Robert of Livonia!" The crowd returned the shout, and one of the tent flaps opened to reveal a middle-aged man wearing a fur robe across his shoulders and a crown atop his head. The fur looked authentic; the crown looked like it came from a dollar store. Allison remembered her own helmet and decided that she shouldn't judge.

There was a smattering of applause and cheering. One lone voice shouted, "Long live the king!" The king looked over in that direction and smiled and waved, then gave a little bow of his head in acknowledgment. Regardless of what his costume looked like, he sure looked like he was reveling in the attention.

"That's the guy," TJ whispered. "The one who owns all this land. Wicked nice when you get to know him. He's like an accountant or a lawyer or something most of the time."

"My people." The king smiled broadly. There was a bit more applause. "MY PEOPLE!" His voice boomed this time, his arms spread out before him. This resulted in more cheering, though one person booed as people fully got into their characters. "My people." His voice was softer now. The crowd edged closer. "These are dark times. Dark times indeed. In years past, our kingdom has cried out when in need of champions, and those among you stepped forward, took up the challenge, and returned victorious. As to the manner in which you approached these challenges . . . well, some were less acceptable to the Crown than others." His eyes fell first upon Chuck, then moved on to several others as he continued. "But we can overlook that in light of your successes." There was a little nervous laughter among the adventurers.

"But those challenges, those trials and tribulations, are but nothing compared to what we now face. A darkness has risen in the East."

TJ chuckled. "It's always the East, isn't it? Sauron, Arawn, the Yankees . . ." The wisecrack spawned considerable laughter, and King Robert scowled in his direction.

"This is no joke, my people. There is a new threat that faces us, and not just us, but all the peoples of our world." Now *that* got people's attention. They were used to plots being based on only local happenings—some barony invading another, or a tribe of goblins passing through and raiding farmers' lands. There were groups all around the country that laid claim to other parts of the world, and each group was mindful not to step on others' toes.

"Word has reached us that a mighty wizard has arisen from the squabbles of the Arcanum in Estervary. We have long been protected here in the West from their internal struggles and from the fallout of their magebattles. This has been partly because of our distance and partly because none wanted to risk looking outward when their power base was still threatened by others.

"But that has all changed. One stands supreme amid the ruins of his rivals and is able to act unchecked—at least for now. He has turned his eyes westward, with thoughts of war and conquest. To be sure, there are many lands and many leagues between Estervary and us, but as each domino falls, he will gain momentum until he is unstoppable."

A voice from the crowd called out, "But what of the rest of the Arcanum? As he moves westward, will they not try to topple him from behind?" It was all Greek to Allison, though it was obvious that most had all the background lore down.

The king nodded. "Indeed, that is always the way of these things. And while yes, history has proven that that is the inevitable conclusion, shall we wait until he has laid waste to our lands and has killed or enslaved our friends and neighbors?" His voice crescendoed. "Or shall we ride forth to meet him, to turn him aside before he comes within a hundred leagues? For myself, and for our people, I choose the latter."

There was a general muttering within the crowd as the assembled heroes digested the information. Allison looked at TJ and said, "Wait, a hundred leagues? Isn't that really incredibly far? Are we going to get on a bus or something? Couldn't they have just emailed us this information beforehand and then pretended we'd already marched by the time we got here?"

He smiled. "Well, that's kind of what we're going to do. After we break camp and head out into the adventure, we'll fast-forward to whatever part of the world holds the next encounter. We won't actually go very far at all, but we'll cross hundreds of miles of game terrain. Willing suspension of disbelief, and all that."

"Like those horns Simon's wearing?"

TJ snorted. "Yeah, exactly."

The murmuring had receded, so their monarch spoke again. "Time is of the essence, my friends. You must proceed with all haste. The fate of not just our lands and people are in your hands, but so is the fate of everyone who lives outside of Estervary. Go now. Go with my blessings, and the blessings of the gods."

With that, the crowd erupted into a cheer. The king gave one last wave before disappearing back into the tent. People began breaking up into small groups, which Allison presumed were their own versions of adventuring parties. She looked around at the boys she was going to be fighting beside for the next two days in their costumes and—in Simon's case—makeup. A surge of adrenaline streamed through her as she convinced herself that she was off to do battle with evil monsters and save the world.

She grinned. "OK, let's go knock some heads." Then she turned toward the woods.

"Wait, Allison," called Simon. "We can't leave quite yet."

"Why not? What about due haste and all that stuff? The fate of the world is in our hands. Shouldn't we get going?"

"Well, yes, and no. Look around. You see all those other parties here?"

Allison counted six other groups. "Um, yes?"

"Well, there aren't enough NPCs—nonplayer characters—for everyone to run off fighting at once. The first group goes out and we give them half an hour, and then the next group goes out and the like. That gives each group time to complete a particular encounter, either killing some monsters or discovering a hidden cache or interviewing a local person, and lets the NPCs set back up for the next group to come through. In the meantime, we just sorta hang out here and shoot the breeze. We can head back into the tavern until our number is called."

Allison nodded, then led the way back to the table they'd left not long before. "For a football player, you sure know an awful lot about how this stuff works."

If he was at all embarrassed, it was well concealed by his makeup. "Yeah, well, it's been a while. Feels good to be back in costume and in character. Back in the saddle, so to speak. I have to say that being Garbaldar"—he pronounced the name with a guttural growl—"sure is a lot of fun. A lot more fun than getting pounded by linebackers. My dad says that Garbaldar won't get me any scholarships for college, though, and being a tailback will. So ol' Garby only comes out every so often."

"Show her your tongue, Garby," Chuck interjected, causing both Jimmy and TJ to laugh, though Stu looked as bemused by the statement as Allison felt.

Simon grinned for a moment and then said, "OK, gimme a second." He turned and fidgeted for a few seconds before turning back around. "Thstand back, folksth," he said and opened his mouth wide, allowing a six-inch tongue to unroll from inside it. He made a slurping noise and waggled it back and forth several times before reaching up and pulling the prosthetic off his real tongue. Allison initially recoiled, but quickly joined in on the laughter.

A voice drifted in from outside the lodge. "Group five, you're up! Group five? Where are you?"

Jimmy jumped up from the table and said, "Whoa, that's us already. They always do it in a random order, and we've *never* gone this quickly. Let's get a move on. I don't want to have the folks behind us hurrying us along. Hey, Allison, did you ever get that mace we were talking about? If not, I've got a spare in my car I can run and grab. She *did* take a proficiency in mace, right?"

TJ nodded. "Yeah, I made sure she took the mace skill, and that she took an armor proficiency too, so she can actually *receive* in-game defensive credit for that truly awesome . . . breastplate"—he snorted—"she's wearing." Allison rolled her eyes at him, but he pretended not to notice. "If you can go grab that mace from your trunk, that'd be great. And then we can get rolling!"

While they waited for Jimmy, the others went to the judge in charge of starting and checked in. He made sure that they matched the descriptions listed on his clipboard and then said, "OK, so here's the scoop. You're going to be traveling through the Duchy of Hanover on your way to Estervary. Just as a reminder, the Hanoverians aren't particularly fond of magic." He looked at TJ. "Or of nonhumans." He looked at Simon. "Head due west into the woods and the adventure will begin. From this point on, coming out of character will cost you experience and treasure rewards, not to mention ruining the fun for everyone else." He consulted his clipboard again and said, "OK, looks like TJ is the group leader." The judge handed him an air horn. "In the case of an out-of-character emergency, blow this three times in rapid succession, and then once every minute afterward so that we can find you. In the case of an in-character emergency, well, I hope you know how to run." He slapped TJ on the butt the way football players often do and winked. "Have fun storming the castle!"

By this time Jimmy had returned with Allison's mace, as well as his own weapon, which was every bit as ridiculous as TJ had led her to believe. The handle was a good foot and a half long, and then the "blade," which was only identifiable as such because it was emerging from the cross guard and painted silver, was another six feet if it was an inch. The foam padding that had been wrapped around the PVC pipe kept it from wobbling too much when it moved, but Allison decided that overall it still looked pretty stupid. It occurred to her, however, that if it was truly the only thing standing between her death at the hands of some power-mad wizard and his assorted minions, she would indulge a little ridiculousness.

She took the mace and hefted it in her hand—it wasn't much more than a stick with a knobby end. Swinging it once or twice, she said, "Thanks. Hold it on this end, whack with that end, and no hits to the head or the, well, you-know-whats, right?"

"Right!" Jimmy gave her an encouraging smile.

"Got it. Let's get moving."

CHAPTER 4

The six headed off in the direction that the starting judge had indicated. Stu took point and Jimmy lagged behind, the two bookending the more pitifully armed and armored party members. Stu had an armband tied to his left arm, which indicated to the NPCs that he had the wilderness ability. Characters who had trained in that ability were less likely to be surprised when traveling in the woods. Any foes they ran into would be sure to make sufficient noise so that the player himself would be warned in time. Groups without such a character would get no added warning, which could be deadly if the monsters carried bows.

The open field gave way to forest, the brilliant fall foliage overhead blocking out much of the sun. The light that made it through to the forest floor was dappled and ephemeral, shifting as the leaves swayed gently in the breeze. Other than the sound of the wind whispering through the branches and the party's footfalls, all was silent. In novels Allison had read, the lack of animal noises always signaled something nasty that had scared the local fauna. But she figured it was just as likely it was their party causing the birds and squirrels to be still as it was some goblins lying in wait.

The friends walked along a rudimentary path that led to one of the campsites farther away from the central lodge. Earlier, Chuck had explained to Allison that, for practical reasons, each adventure typically covered roughly the same area of the nature reserve. None of the organizers had the time or inclination to create brand-new paths and structures every time. The stories changed, of course, and how the terrain was used varied from weekend to weekend, but they had walked down this very path several times before.

Suddenly, Stu raised his fist. Everyone stumbled to a stop and looked wildly around for danger. Chuck held his dagger at the ready, and TJ casually opened his beanbag pouch to prepare to cast a spell. Jimmy inched closer to the rest of the group, his sword raised and ready to strike. Everyone's ears strained to catch any sounds.

When no danger materialized, Stu's hand dropped back down, and he began moving forward once again. Not three steps later, a cough rang out from beside the path, and he spun, his bow drawn and aimed at a nearby bush.

A cackling voice called out, "Don't shoot! Don't shoot! Unarmed and friendly-like, I am. You see me, yes?"

"See you?" Allison smirked. "Well, you're still hiding behind that bush, so it's kinda hard to see much of anything."

The voice replied, "Come out, can I? Or shoot me and smite me will you, and leave my poor Wilfred without a father?"

With a long look back along the path, Jimmy moved forward to stand protectively between the bushes and the rest of the party. Stu's bow was still drawn, but he looked inquiringly at the others.

TJ cleared his voice and called out, "Yes, you can come out, if you mean us no harm. But be aware that if you act in a hostile manner toward us, it will go all the worse for you."

"Oh yes, great master. Yes, kind I will be. And polite. And friendly-like. Oh yes!" The voice sounded to Allison like a cross between Gollum and Yoda. A head peeked out of the bush, followed quickly by the rest of the creature. The young man playing the character wore a grotesque mask that sported a long nose and bushy eyebrows, and he wore a generic brown robe that covered his entire body.

"Goblin," TJ murmured to Allison. "Not a serious threat to us unless he has a couple dozen more hiding among the trees. However, they're devious and are not to be trusted."

The goblin turned to look at TJ and said, "Oh, not to be trusted, are we? Who the land beside the Lake of Dreams they promised to give us, and then their mind they changed? Hmm? Who the crafts and other pretty things of the Bonecrusher clan they promised to buy, and then on pain of death just took them? Hmm? Who the devious ones are, hmm? Not the Bonecrushers, for sure that is." He then turned and stared directly at Simon. "The truth about who is the more devious, your people know, don't they? Eh?"

Simon looked ready to speak, but TJ interrupted. "Yeah, well, it's true those events were unfortunate. But none of us had a hand in them. You should have no quarrel with us. Speak your piece and then be gone."

"Oh, speak my piece, eh? Well, here is the *peace* I am speaking. Danger in these woods there is. Greater danger than the Bonecrusher clan has ever seen. Greater danger than the Bonecrusher clan ever wants to see. If on this path you continue, an unfortunate doom you will meet. But if that doom you meet and overcome, earn the friendship of the Bonecrusher clan you will, as well as any shinies we may have." The goblin began cackling madly but after several seconds fell into a coughing fit. Waving, he stepped back into the shadows of the bushes.

"Wait! Can't you tell us anything more?" asked Chuck. But by that point the creature was completely hidden from view.

A moment later the robed figure was back, but this time he wore a judge's armband rather than the goblin's mask. He looked blankly at the group and said, "The goblin has disappeared." His transition from goblin to game official indicated that this particular NPC was no longer in play for their party.

The six looked at each other briefly before Allison said with a sigh, "Well, that was ominous, but not terribly informative. I guess we just keep moving and see what happens?"

Chuck looked at her and said, "Oh no, I don't think we're quite through here yet." He approached the judge and showed him one of the skill chits attached to his carabiner. "I search the area, particularly the bushes where he had been hiding."

The judge smiled and said, "Aha. Well, as it happens, with that many ranks, in your search you spot something glinting on the ground. Upon closer inspection, you find this. You're lucky—we hadn't really expected anyone to be able to spot that. Assists wouldn't have helped." Looking at TJ, the judge said, "Galphalon's a wizard, right?" At TJ's nod, he handed a laminated three-by-five note card and a purple armband to Chuck, then concluded with, "There is nothing else for you to see here. It's time to move on." This was a none-too-subtle hint that they should be out of sight before the next group came behind so as not to ruin the experience for them.

Chuck gave the note card a quick glance and emitted a low whistle. "Good stuff, folks. Let's get moving, and everyone can take a look at it on the way." He shot a jealous glance at Allison.

"You are one lucky little newbie. Wait till you see what you get to play with!" He handed her the armband and said, "Put that on right away." Despite the confused look on her face, she did as he instructed.

Stu gave the card only a brief glance before resuming his position as scout, but he was grinning when he handed it to TJ.

As TJ read over the card, he said, "Whoa, yeah. Chuckles was right about this one. Check this thing out." He handed it to Allison.

"What's it say?" Jimmy called out from behind. He had resumed his position as rear guard and was anxiously looking into the trees, sword still at the ready. The encounter with the goblin hadn't taken very long, so there could very well be an ambush set up ahead. "I want to know what it is too!"

Allison read the card aloud. "'Ring of Ancient Triumph. One of the magical implements created during the third age of the Ny'Zull dynasty by the master dwarven craftsman Dylan Bloodforge.' Good grief, there is a lot of exposition here. How are we supposed to know all that?"

TJ answered, "That's why he asked if I was a wizard, as opposed to some other spellcaster, like a mage or a sorcerer. It is assumed that as part of my studies I have learned all sorts of history about magic from past ages. If I hadn't been here, he would have given us a different card, which wouldn't have included any of the backstory and might not have even told us anything about the ring's power. But keep reading—you haven't gotten to the good part.

She continued: "'This ring was crafted for the High Autarch of the Ny'Zull's religion and can only be worn by one who channels divine power.' I guess that's me, right?"

TJ nodded and winked.

"'As the ultimate conduit between the Heavens and the priesthood, the High Autarch was expected to manifest the gods' power for all the people to see. When the Ny'Zull pantheon began to wane during the Godswar, the High Autarch commissioned this ring to be made as a way to bolster his weakening power. The wearer of this ring is granted the following abilities:

"'One, five extra spellcasts each day, of any spell rank.' Whoa. That doubles the number of spells I've got. I bet I won't be running out of those heals on you after all, will I?

"'Two, the power of the ring encases the wearer in a magical shell that reduces the effectiveness of enemy weapons, mundane and magical. This effectively increases the wearer's armor rating by six points and negates any magical effects projected by enemy weapons.' That sounds cool enough.

"'Three, the ring radiates an aura of majesty that influences the way others see the wearer. All reactions will be shifted positively by one tier, and all creatures of rank three or lower are awed by the bearer—they will defend themselves if provoked, but will not attack of their own volition.' Now *that* is cool. Any of you guys lower than rank four? If so, you may begin bowing down in front of me now." She turned a pirouette and dipped into a deep curtsy.

"Nope, sorry, Allison," Simon said with a chuckle. "None of us are threes. But Chuck wasn't kidding. That ring has no business being in the hands of a newbie. They must have figured that if someone in the party had sufficient search skill to find it, anyone capable of wearing it would also be a pretty high level. That's the sort of thing you'll probably never see again in-game. None of us have anything that rivals it in power. Unless you do, Stu."

"Nope, not me. Just my trusty bow."

Chuck let out a laugh. "You know what this means, Allison, don't you?"

"What?"

"You're going to have to keep coming back to play."

"Why's that?"

"Because if word gets out that an item like that went to a first-timer who never came back, you're going to have people egging your house for years to come."

"Yeah, well, we'll see. This is turning out to be more fun than I expected."

The snap of a twig was the only warning they had before all hell broke loose.

CHAPTER 5

It began with a flight of arrows from the bushes to the left of the path. Everyone knew that the missiles—identical to the ones Stu carried, with large padded heads—were unlikely to actually hurt anyone, but the effect was no less startling.

A guttural voice shouted, "Arrows, two points!" and Jimmy and Chuck, both of whom had been hit, called back, "Arrow hit, minus two points." Three other arrows missed their mark, sailing harmlessly over Allison's and TJ's heads. The six friends hastily retreated behind some trees, and a second round of arrows bounced off their cover.

The voice called out again. "Surrender, or die painfully!"

Allison looked over at the others and shrugged. Peeking her head out from behind the tree, she replied, "And what happens if we surrender?"

As soon as her face was visible, a third flight of arrows flew across the path, all targeted at her. Her eyes grew wide and she ducked back with a squeak. Luckily, they all passed by.

"What about my stupid ring?" she complained.

"Must be level fours." TJ shrugged. "Just keep ducking."

Stu, who had gotten his bow out, fired an arrow of his own toward the bushes. "Magic arrow, seven points, accuracy skill mark two!" he shouted.

The arrow got caught in the bushes and hung their limply. Nonetheless, a figure stepped out from them on the other side and called, "Accuracy hit, seven damage, dead." He then proceeded to stagger back and forth several times before falling to the ground with a dramatic groan.

Stu grinned wolfishly. "Cool, huh? A new skill I picked up with my last rank. I'm only able to do it twice a day, though, and I'd rather not blow my second one now in a lame ambush encounter. Not that they necessarily know that, do they?" Then he shouted, "Go ahead, do that again. Lemme see where you're hiding."

There were several moments of tense silence before the sound of voices in grunted conversation drifted across the distance. Suddenly, four bodies charged from the bushes and toward the trees where the friends crouched. Their foes were dressed all in brown and wore wolf masks. Having left their bows behind, the wolf men brandished short padded weapons that looked to be either clubs or swords, though Allison couldn't be sure which. Given her newness at the game and how fragile her character was, she figured it didn't really matter which. Whether she got stabbed or beaten to death, the end result was the same.

Stu released another arrow, again calling out, "Magic arrow, seven points," this time without the accuracy skill.

The arrow flew true, and the monster struck in the chest said, "Arrow hit, seven damage, dead." Then he fell over like his friend, mimicking the over-the-top death sequence.

Jimmy, knowing that his enormous sword was of no use among the trees, leapt out to meet them on open ground before they could close the full distance. Swinging his blade wildly over his head, he roared, "Magic flamberge, ten points!"

The three remaining enemies, seeing his berserker headband, immediately converged upon him and tried to dodge within the radius of his swings. Clearly concerned about Stu's archery, they kept to the far side of the path in the hope that Jimmy would provide them cover from arrows.

Each of the wolf men announced, "Club, two damage," and began swinging their weapons at Jimmy, but none were able to get close enough to score on him. Allison suddenly realized why the other boys had been so happy about the giant sword. It seemed unlikely that any enemies would be able to get close enough to strike him so long as he was paying attention. The only way they'd be able to bring him down would be if they gang rushed him. Two would certainly die, but the third might be able to do some damage.

Stu let loose a third arrow, which passed dangerously close to Jimmy.

"Cut that out!" Jimmy shouted, and Stu dropped his bow with a sigh.

Unfortunately, Stu had spent so many skill points on archery, his melee and armor skills were next to useless. Because of this, rather than charging into the fray with the sword he had drawn, he hung back in the hope that Jimmy would mop them up alone.

Chuck, on the other hand, was eager to put his new skill point in daggers to use and stepped out of the woods with his weapon drawn. Jimmy's weapon was still whistling back and forth, keeping the wolf men's attention, so Chuck circled around to engage their enemies from behind. He planned to set up a flanking position and end the battle quickly.

TJ turned to Allison. "Stay put. You're no good to us dead." Then he stepped out from the trees. "Magic missile!" he shouted, narrowly missing one of their enemies with a thrown beanbag.

Simon joined, threw a beanbag of his own at Jimmy's feet, and called out, "Curse enemy. Minus two to all damage." The wolf men looked dismayed, and Jimmy pressed the attack. If their clubs could do only two damage points in the first place, and they all suffered a minus two on each hit, then now their strikes would be ineffectual. They turned to run, but by that time Chuck had circled around them, and the two boys made quick work of their foes.

When the NPCs had removed their masks and donned their judge armbands, Chuck again told them his search skill rank, and he was given a card indicating that they had found some small coins but nothing else of real value. Not even the weapons were worth keeping—it turned out those clubs were just the leg bones of some unfortunate past dinners and the bows were equally junky. Meanwhile, Stu retrieved the arrows he had fired and placed them back in his quiver.

Allison flashed Simon a smile and said, "That was a nice trick there, though kinda anticlimactic. How come there's nothing to show for it but those coins?"

"That, my friend, is what we call an Obligatory Thug Attack, and there's usually something along these lines in each adventure. It's not important to the plot, and there's no real life-threatening danger, but the hope is that it makes the party use up some of its resources early, so when we run into something more challenging we aren't at full power. For instance, both TJ and I blew a spell, and though I don't disagree with

Stu's use of his accuracy ability, that's the sort of thing that could really come in handy later. We took a little damage, but that's really not a big deal, particularly with a healer handy."

TJ interjected, "Though if we hadn't had Stu and his bow, we might have found ourselves in a very different situation. If I'd been setting this up, I'd have had another group ready to come at us from behind in the event that we hid behind the trees. For all we know, they're still out there, but when they saw what we did to their friends, they melted back into the forest. I agree that this was mostly just a nuisance, but it could very easily have turned into something worse."

Simon nodded and continued. "As for loot, don't get spoiled by that ring we found. Most encounters don't give much of anything. I mean, think about it. These wolf men jumped a bunch of armed adventurers. They were probably pretty desperate."

"Well, one thing's for sure," said Jimmy. "This isn't an ordinary weekend adventure. Between Allison's ring and the fact that they jumped us so quickly after the first encounter, this looks like it's going to be way more intense than usual. I expected to have a good half hour of traveling before we ran into a fight. We're going to have to keep a much closer eye out for more ambushes as we go. It may even be worth moving off the path and into the woods as we march. It'll be a bit slower going, but much safer."

Stu nodded. "I agree. I like walking in the woods anyway. It's peaceful."

There were no objections, so the group set off once again. As predicted, they weren't able to move as quickly as when they were on the path. Low bushes, while not dense, still grabbed at them, and fallen branches and logs provided obstacles for them to go around or climb over.

"Maybe this wasn't such a good idea after all," Chuck panted as he straddled yet another of the fallen logs.

"Yeah, this may have been a mistake," agreed Simon. "Garby may be a nature sprite, but I for one would much rather be running across an open field."

"Even pounded by linebackers?" quipped TJ.

Simon barked a laugh. "No, definitely not. This is way more fun and less painful. I run track in the spring, though. No tackles then."

"Two-season athlete?" Stu asked, impressed. "I never really got the hang of organized sports."

"Three, actually," Simon replied. "Dad's got me in basketball in the winter. Says athletics are a year-round pursuit nowadays. Summers I'm off to camps too."

"Wow." Allison put a hand on Simon's shoulder. "Sounds like your dad is just as wound up now as he was coaching us way back when."

"Eh," came the reply. "I guess." Simon pulled ahead a few steps and fell silent. Each of the friends retreated into their own thoughts.

A large bramble patch required them to make a wide detour, and for a time the path disappeared completely from view. None of them wanted to get lost in the woods and have to use the air horn to call for help, so they fell silent and concentrated on getting through it. When they did finally find the trail again, they gave up being sneaky and stuck to the open ground. The sky darkened as clouds passed in front of the sun, and the path took on a grayish hue. An unfamiliar trill floated through the air, answered by another in the distance. Everyone in the group froze and crouched instinctively, fearing another ambush. The calls repeated twice, but there was no visible motion on either side of the path. Stu held up a hand, pointed to himself, and made a walking motion with his fingers.

As he crept forward, his eyes scanned left and right for any sign of danger. The ground beneath his feet was covered by a soft layer of pine needles and moss, so he made no sound as he moved. The birds called back and forth once more, and again he froze, eyes squinting. A light breeze passed through the trees, and the leaves rattled. Up above, he spotted a flash of red, and this time the trill was accompanied by the sound of flapping wings receding into the distance.

The tension drained and he stood up from his crouch. "Looks like it's all clear, guys. Really was a bird. Never seen one of those before. Must be migratory or something." He shrugged. "Let's get moving again and see what's up next. I can't imagine that the doom the crazy goblin predicted was that little ambush. We should try picking up the pace."

The group all agreed with Stu's assessment, and off they went again, moving a bit more quickly to make up for the time they had lost detouring around the brambles. At some point, wagon ruts appeared on the path they were following.

"Nice touch," TJ remarked when he noticed it. "I wonder how long it took them to get those put in. Must have taken quite a while."

"Eh," replied Chuck. "We had that rain last weekend. I bet it made the ground all nice and muddy."

About twenty minutes later, they began to detect signs of other people. The scent of a wood fire drifted toward them on the light breeze, and in the distance they could hear the sound of voices. The path bent slightly to the right, and when they rounded the bend they came upon a small settlement. There were half a dozen ramshackle cottages clumped together along one side of the path. Between several of the buildings were makeshift roofs, under which some scrawny-looking goats had taken shelter.

Two small children were playing with sticks in the dirt alongside the path, oblivious to the approaching friends. The six stepped out fully into the clearing, and Stu cleared his throat loudly. The children looked up and squawked in alarm before running into one of the houses. One of them shouted, "Maw! Paw! Soldiers!" The door slammed behind them, leaving the adventurers turning to each other in surprise.

Moments later, a man in his mid- to late twenties emerged from the house, angrily brandishing a pitchfork. A woman's head peered out through the cracked door. "What are you folks doin' here?" the man asked. "We don't need or want your kind here. Go on, now. Git."

"Quiet, Claude," hissed the woman through the doorway. "Remember what happened to ol' Clem. Just give 'em what they want and ask 'em to move on. We don't want no trouble."

The man—Claude, evidently—spit a glob of phlegm on the ground and grumbled, "Naw, we don't want no trouble. But we don't want none o' what you folks are peddlin' either. You wanna take my goats this time? Or my kids? How 'bout you just slit my throat and be done with it? You're just about there as it is. Hmm?"

Stu looked around helplessly, clearly out of his element. Simon stepped forward and spoke in soft tones. "Hello, sir. Claude, is it? It is good to meet you, friend."

"You're no friend of mine, ya pointy-headed freak. You or the other one, wherever he's from." He nodded toward Stu, who stood with mouth suddenly agape at the obvious reference to his brown skin. "You ain't welcome here. Now git." The woman in the doorway cringed.

Exchanging a glance with Stu, but deciding to ignore the slights, Simon continued. "We may not be friends yet, but that's simply because we haven't met." He smiled and nodded at the rhyme. "I think that you have mistaken us for someone else. We mean you no harm, and we certainly don't want any of your livestock. Or anything of yours, except perhaps information. We are simply travelers passing through, and we have stumbled upon your town. It is still early yet, and we plan on moving on soon."

"That's what your kind always says. You're just passing through. You don't mean any harm. Well, here's what I have to say to that!" He coughed up another loogie and spit just in front of Simon's feet.

Simon looked around for backup. TJ and Chuck exchanged glances and shrugged.

At last Allison sighed and said, "Are we really gonna be stopped here by some angry pitchfork-wielding peasant who is at best not going to tell us anything and at worst deranged?"

The man shot a look at Allison, and a visible change came over him. His eyes widened, his jaw grew slightly slack, and he knuckled his forehead. "M-m-milady," he said. "I didn't see you standin' there until just now." He stood up straighter and said in a more measured tone, "Please forgive my gruffness. We have suffered much at the hands of outlaws pretendin' to be the king's soldiers. And at the hands of the king's soldiers pretendin' to be outlaws."

Simon and Stu both looked at Allison in amazement, until they remembered the armband she was wearing that signified the powers of her ring.

Without missing a beat, Allison replied, "There is nothing to forgive, my good man. These are troubling times, and it is important for you to stand up for your home and your family."

"Thank you, my lady." He bowed to her, then half turned to face the house. "C'mon, woman! Put a kettle on and brew up some tea for Her Ladyship and her servants!"

TJ smirked and muttered, "Servants? Really?"

"Shush," replied Allison quietly. "Let the poor man believe what he wishes. It's certainly a better reception than before, so just go with it."

During this exchange, some of the other villagers had emerged from their own dwellings, and a sorry lot they were. It quickly became clear why Claude alone had stood up to them—no one else was in any position to help. The next youngest was easily thirty years older than Claude and walked with a crutch under his left shoulder. The hair on all the rest had long gone gray. Any one of the party—including Allison—could have beaten them single-handedly. Each one, as they approached, nodded in Allison's direction, and the woman's peering face in the crack of the door had been replaced by those of the two children.

"So can you tell us what has been bothering you of late?" Simon tried engaging the man in conversation once again. "We fought and dispatched some wolf men not so long ago. If they were troubling you, they are no more, and you can now live in peace."

"Wolf men? Here?" There was a flutter of discussion and panicked looks on their faces. "No, there ain't been none of them here since my great-grandpa's time. If you really saw some in these woods, 'tis dark news indeed. We have had a hard enough time scratchin' for a livin' with only other men to contend with, not nature's freaks." He had the grace to blush, then bobbed his head toward Simon. "Milady's companions not included, of course."

He paused before continuing. "We have long been at the mercy of the brigands who pass through these woods. And when the soldiers come from the king, they are just as bad. Ain't no justice to be gotten from them. Everyone takes from us; they are all the same."

Allison's face softened. "Well, why do you stay, then? Couldn't you find somewhere safer to live?"

"My good wife and me and our children could move. But where could we go? Our only livin' is to sell our meager wares to travelers and occasionally provide them shelter for the night. I ain't got no plow, no mule, and no knowledge of farming. Perhaps we could become beggars in some town, though I don't believe it would be any less dangerous for us to do so. And even if the four of us did leave, some here don't have that sort of travelin' in 'em. I can't desert these people. They've been my friends all my life."

"If you have so little, why do the brigands continue to harass you?"

"'Cause they can." The statement was simple, yet powerful.

Jimmy spoke up. "Well, as it happens, we are pretty good at giving brigands serious beatdowns. Perhaps this is something we could help you with. Where do they live, and just how many are there?"

Claude cocked his head in confusion at Jimmy's suggestion, then shrugged. "Usually there are fewer than a dozen. But even a half-dozen well-armed men are more than a match for the likes of us. They come from the north, through the woods, though it is possible they are attemptin' to hide their tracks. I doubt it, though. They are brash enough and know we can't do nothin' about it."

One of the children peeked out from behind his mother's skirts. "Their camp really is up north, and not too far. Only a couple hours' walk or so, if you hurry."

The woman shushed him and tried to push him back behind her, but Claude replied, "You tellin' fibs again, Fin? How should you know where they are?"

"'Cause I followed 'em once, Paw. I'm real quick and real quiet too. Remember that time I got lost and you found me wandering in the woods?" He blushed lightly and scuffed the ground with a foot. "I had followed 'em all the way to their camp and then came back. I'd thought I could sneak back into bed, but when I heard you callin' my name I knew I was gonna get caught, so I pretended that I'd gotten lost. I sure am sorry, Paw."

The child's mother looked horrified, and she immediately shooed him back into their hovel. Her raised voice drifted through the walls, and though her words were unclear, her tone most certainly was not.

Claude just shook his head grimly. "Well, there you have it, strangers. You wanna find 'em, that's the direction you should head. Not that I can really see why you'd go outta your way for us. We ain't got nothing to repay you with."

An awkward silence hung for just a moment before Allison said, "You don't need to repay us with anything but your gratitude. We'll see an end to these brigands so that you can live your lives in peace."

If she was expecting a joyous reaction from the townsfolk, she was deeply disappointed. They looked at her with blank faces, devoid of optimism.

Claude replied, "Well, ma'am, if you say so, we'd be much obliged to you," then left it at that. Evidently the charm of the ring only went so far. It might convince them that she was an important person, but it couldn't convince them that she was at all interested in improving their meager lot in life. It also didn't convince them to provide any assistance, whether food or guidance. "North, only a couple hours' walk or so" was the extent of it.

Simon looked at Claude and said, "Is there anything else you'd like to tell us? I've a plus four in diplomatic interactions."

The man simply stared at him for a few moments, then turned his back. "OK, folks, let 'em go about their business, and let's go about our own. We sure got plenty to do as it is." This was met with muttered acquiescence as the crowd dispersed. It wasn't long before the six friends were standing alone on the path, their only company the eye of one of the children peering through a knothole in the plank wall of his house.

"Guess a plus four wasn't good enough to get anything, though it usually is. Anyway, what do you guys think we should do? This is clearly a side quest, but it wouldn't surprise me if there's something juicy at the end of it. They wouldn't have us tramping a couple hours off the path for no benefit, and it looks like they really spent a lot of work building up these houses and stuff. You want to go fight some brigands, or head off to fight whatever foozle that goblin warned us about?"

"I want to know what the hell that 'other one' comment was about," muttered Stu, making air quotes with his fingers. "I'm pretty sure I'm not paying to field insults like that."

"That's not normal?" asked Allison.

"Not out here," he replied, fists clenched. "Never where I could hear it, at least."

TJ shook his head. "Yeah, that was bizarre. Some things you just don't say, even in the context of being in character. But I didn't recognize that actor. Maybe he's new and too gung ho with the racial stereotypes of the time? He sure had Simon pegged."

Jimmy patted Stu on the shoulder. "We'll get it all sorted out when we get back to the lodge tonight. Don't let one jerk ruin the whole weekend for you."

The archer heaved a sigh. "OK, fine. I'll let it go for now. But that wasn't cool. And doesn't solve the problem of what to do next."

Chuck was first to answer. "Well, you know my stance on things. Brigands mean loot. I'm all for it."

Stu nodded. "I agree. I could use the XP and can't stand knowing there are folks up to no good in the forest. That's two strong reasons in favor of it."

"Sounds like we're all in agreement," TJ concluded. "A quick detour to bang some heads and grab some loot, and we'll be back on track in no time!"

After one last look around they set off through the trees. While there wasn't a path per se, there was clear evidence that people had been passing through that area. Stu noticed a couple footprints in dried mud, and he pointed out places where small branches had been snapped sideways, as someone walking past them might do.

"Well, that stands to reason," said Chuck. "The NPCs had to head this direction, as did the group in front of us, so the way should be pretty obvious."

What was surprising was how long the journey became. As TJ had explained to Allison earlier, long trips were typically shortened into fifteen- or twenty-minute walks representing days of travel. After they had walked for an hour with no visible signs of any bad guys, the group started to become restless.

"Man, did we take a wrong turn or something?" Chuck grumbled. "They couldn't have just sent us on a wild-goose chase, could they? If so, I'm gonna ask for my money back, 'cause this is seriously not fun." Then, in his best Bugs Bunny voice: "Maybe we shoulda taken that left at Albuquerque." He groaned and sat down against a tree, then took out his water skin and had a long drink. "And my feet are starting to bug me. I'm not used to this tramping about in the woods. I'd much rather have nice cobbled streets under my feet."

Allison looked at Chuck sympathetically. Her breastplate was starting to get heavy on her, but she knew she couldn't drop it. Her uncle was expecting it to be returned to the theater on Sunday night, in the same condition he'd lent it. She didn't look forward to explaining why it was damaged or missing and then having to chip in to replace it.

Stu shook his head. "No, we didn't miss a turn. I'm sure of that. Look over here." He pointed to something on the ground. "Do you see how that moss is pressed against the ground there? This sort of moss typically has a much greater volume when it grows wild. The fact that it's crushed means that someone or something stepped on it. We haven't lost the trail—we just haven't walked far enough yet."

"Whoa," said Jimmy. "You just made that up, didn't you?"

"Nah, of course not. I've spent years in woods just like these, learning the lay of the land. With all those brothers and sisters at home, I needed to get away a lot. I was never much for sports and really like the peace and quiet out here." After a pause he continued. "I haven't spent much time in this particular area, of course, but I recognize that moss. It's called greybeard. Grows all over the place. It's actually something you can make a nutritious soup out of, though I think you'd have to be pretty hard up to eat it."

Allison grimaced. "Greybeard soup, huh. How appetizing."

Stu laughed and extended a hand to Chuck, hoisting him from where he sat. "Come on, friend. Let's get moving. The sooner we get there the sooner we can give them a solid drubbing and find out what sort of loot they've got. And maybe even grab a bite to eat."

There was vigorous head nodding at the prospect of finding food, and so the party once again set off, following Stu's lead. In places, he pointed out other markings that suggested people had passed through. At times Simon nodded at what Stu pointed out, but the other four simply looked on dumbly, hoping that he wasn't just making things up as they walked. Another hour passed and Chuck began complaining about his feet again. Stu cut him off with a quick *"Shh."* Chuck gave him a pained look, but bit back his reply.

Stu glanced back from where he was leading and said, "Do you hear that?"

The other five looked blankly at each other and shrugged.

"Nope," said TJ.

"Really? I hear voices ahead. They sound so loud to me."

Chuck groaned. "You better not be pulling our legs, Stu. I don't think I could stand the disappointment of more walking."

"No, I'm sure of it. You all stay here, and I'll be back in a few. I'm going to go see what I can see." Without waiting for an answer, he slipped off into the woods, quickly disappearing from view. The friends looked at each other in confusion, and Chuck flopped back down on the ground to rub his feet. "This greybeard is pretty comfy to sit on, in addition to making a nutritious soup." He chuckled, and the others smiled as they sat down too.

Long minutes dragged on before Stu finally returned to their resting spot. He gave them a grim look and said, "They're only a couple minutes away. Like Claude said, there looks to be fewer than ten. But they seem to know what they're doing. Their camp is picketed with sharp stakes, and they have at least one lookout. There's no way I'll be able to pick them off with my bow, so it's got to be melee. And I don't suppose that any of them will be rank three or lower, so our dear healer won't be able to wow them with her ring."

The report left the group in silence for a time, until Jimmy spoke up. "Well, we've fought two-to-one odds before. It's not easy, but it's not impossible. And of course we've got some magic on our side that I'm sure our enemies don't. Wizards don't go around shaking down peasants for bags of turnips. I say we give it a whirl and see what happens."

This made sense to the rest of the group. Chuck seemed the one most interested in the fight, since he wanted to justify the long walk. Allison was wary of the numbers disadvantage, since they were counting on her to contribute. The last battle she'd just scooched back and hid, and she had been looking forward to doing that again.

"C'mon and live a little," Jimmy said, enthused. "So maybe we'll take a little damage. Or even a lot. No big deal! We've got you, and you've got me!"

"Well, what if I'm the one who takes a lot of damage? I distinctly remember TJ saying I couldn't take much." She looked anxiously at the other four.

Simon patted her on the arm. "Don't worry. You'll be fine. Just keep Jimmy between you and any bad guys, and it will all work out."

"Exactly," Jimmy said, piling on. "I'm tough enough to take care of all of you!"

"And anyway," chipped in Chuck, "she's a newbie! She doesn't really know what's going on anyway, so it's not like she really even gets a vote."

The boys all laughed, and Allison had a hard time refuting the assertion, so she shrugged and agreed.

The group slowly crept through the forest toward the brigand camp. As they got closer, they all began to hear the voices Stu had pointed out earlier. It was a mixture of boastful oaths and drunken song—it appeared that they had recently returned from roving, no doubt shaking down another pathetic group of peasants. Within a few minutes the party had arrived at the edge of a clearing, in the center of which was a rudimentary military camp. As Stu had said, there was a wooden palisade around the camp, and one of the brigands walked the perimeter, looking out into the trees.

"So how are we going to do this?" asked Jimmy. "Charge the entrance and fight hand to hand inside? We can't wait for dark, can we? If there's another group or three behind us, we don't have the luxury to wait around a couple hours. Even if only one other group decides to come this direction, they'll be here well before dusk."

There was much head nodding. "Well, let's go around and take a look at the front door and see what there is to see," said Allison. "I still don't have the best feeling about this, but if we're going to do it, we should do it right."

Stu led them a quarter of the way around, following the direction of the sentry so that they were always just behind his field of vision. They discovered that the entrance was little more than an open space in the wall of stakes, and there was a single guard standing watch there, though he looked bored with his duty.

"Perfect, a sleepy sentry at the gate and one walking the perimeter," said Jimmy. He looked pleased. "If we time our movement so he's on the opposite side, that will be one less we need to deal with at the outset. With luck I'll be able to take out several of them before he's able to come back around and join the fight. That should help even the odds a bit. And once we've gotten in, Stu can always take that one out with his bow."

It wasn't the most brilliant of tactical plans, but everyone agreed that it would do the trick. The group shifted around another eighth of the circle so they were out of direct view of the guard at the gate. They hoped to make it all the way to him before he saw them. Ideally, they'd be able to cut him down before he could raise the alarm.

Just as the roving sentry passed around the curve of the fence and out of sight, the six ran at a crouch across the clearing to the wall. No leaves had blown into the area, so their treads were silent on the soft grass. Hugging the wall, they slowly crept toward the open gate and the unsuspecting sentry.

"Hey! What's that? Intruders!" A voice rang out through the clearing, and all six heads snapped around and looked toward the trees. A man stood there, a bow in hand and a deer draped across his shoulders. He shrugged the carcass off and calmly placed an arrow to his bow. He released the string, and the arrow streaked across the distance, striking Simon squarely in the chest.

"Oof," he wheezed as the air was compressed from his lungs. He leaned against the wall, dazed, blinking slowly as he looked down and saw the arrow—a real arrow—protruding from his chest, blood slowly trickling out. Pain shot through his body. His eyes rolled back in his head, and he sank into merciful oblivion.

CHAPTER 6

"What the . . . ?" was all TJ was able to say before he realized that the archer was nocking another arrow to his bow. "Run! *Now!*" he shouted, herding his friends toward the opening in the fence and away from the open ground.

"What about Simon?" Allison asked, hesitating.

"Leave him for now. We've got to move or we're all dead. That madman will skewer us all!" TJ pulled on her sleeve.

Jerking her arm from his grasp, Allison grabbed at Simon's collar and gave a tug, but there was no way she could move him. A sudden force spun her around. The second arrow had struck her in the shoulder. But by some miracle it had been deflected into the palisade wall, where it now stuck, quivering. Choking back a cry of despair, she turned and fled after the others.

As she darted through the entrance to the fort, Allison found her four friends backed against one of the inside walls, the previously bored-looking guard brandishing his sword at them. They had their hands raised in front of them in submission, but the man didn't seem likely to grant them mercy. Unsure what to do, she reached for the mace hanging from a strap on her belt. It had more heft to it than one would expect from foam-wrapped PVC pipe. Instinctively, she crossed the distance and swung it with all her strength at the back of the guard's head. It made a sickening smack that reminded her of the time she and some other kids got together after Halloween to crush jack-o'-lanterns with baseball bats. The guard heaved forward and landed at the feet of his captives.

The four froze for a moment, looking back and forth between Allison and the crumpled body lying still in front of them. The back of the guard's head was crushed in, and fluid leaked out. He was clearly not breathing. He was clearly dead.

"Oh my god, oh my god, oh my god, oh my god" was all that Allison could bring herself to say. Her knees buckled beneath her, and TJ stepped forward to hold her up. Their eyes connected, and she saw in his something she had never seen before: a sense of knowledge, or perhaps understanding, that hadn't been there at school the day before.

But there was no time for that. Breaking eye contact, Allison looked around to find the inside of the compound consisted of a half-dozen or so separate buildings, several with smoke drifting lazily from chimneys. A central path led from the entrance toward a garden against the back wall. The other three had moved away from the opening in the wall to put the bulk of the nearest building between them and the rest of the compound. With Allison leaning against TJ's shoulder, the two staggered away from the fort's entrance to join their friends, who waited against the inside of the palisade wall.

Once there, with his free hand, TJ reached for the air horn they had been given in case of emergencies. When it was securely in his grasp, he raised it to his mouth and blew with all his might. The horn rang out for several seconds before he pulled it from his lips in bewilderment. Rather than finding what the judge had given him, he grasped an actual horn of some animal, its closed end carved into a mouthpiece. In response to the sound, rough voices from deeper inside the compound called out in confusion.

Springing into action, Stu reached to grab his bow off his back and was curiously unsurprised to discover that it was no longer a piece of fiberglass but rather a long, curved piece of yew with a well-waxed string. Without thinking, he leaned into the wood, stringing the bow smoothly. He raised it with one hand and drew an arrow from his quiver with a smooth motion.

Stepping back out through the palisade gate, he pulled back the nocked arrow to his cheek and scanned for more enemies. The archer who had shot Simon was waiting for just such an opportunity, and let fly. The missile flew toward Stu, but an errant breeze blew it off course, and it embedded in the wall to his right.

Sounds of other brigands coming to investigate floated across the wind, but Stu ignored them. Instead, he tracked the arrow's trajectory to the archer in the woods and released his own string. His arrow sped across the clearing and hit the archer in his neck, just above his studded leather chest piece. The brigand reached up to stanch the flow of his lifeblood as he fell slowly to his knees. Then he slumped dead to the ground. Stu calmly turned toward the center of the compound, drew a second arrow, and set it to flight just as quickly. It too found its mark, catching one of their enemies in the chest as he turned a corner, sword raised to charge. Pivoting, he shot again, and his third arrow found the sentry who had been patrolling the compound's exterior. Drawing yet another, Stu strode deeper into the compound and around a corner with a look of determination on his face.

Jimmy had unslung his sword from its harness. Six feet of wickedly sharpened serpentine steel glinted in front of him, and he swung it experimentally several times. It felt as if he'd been born with it in his hand, as if it were designed for him personally. He let out a whoop and shouted, "Come and git some!" Chuck, with a look of anxiety on his face, followed behind his larger friend and disappeared from Allison's view.

Three brigands who had come to investigate the shouting saw Jimmy charging at them and turned to look for somewhere to run. One ran left, one ran right, and the third just stood there as Jimmy bore down on him. The man drew his sword and held it in front of him, but the look on his face made it clear he was more used to harassing peasants than facing off against other trained fighters.

Jimmy swung his sword high, putting the entire weight of his body behind the strike. The blow was deflected to the side, but the impact drove his opponent backward a step. As Jimmy's follow-through spun him full circle, he brought the sword down low, slicing just under the brigand's raised sword. The magically sharp blade parted his foe's armor like a hot knife through butter, and a bright red line appeared across the villain's midsection. He dropped his sword with a grunt and doubled over, his hands trying desperately to hold his wound closed. Jimmy followed the slice with a boot to the head, and the man crumpled to the ground. With a laugh, he turned left and sprinted after one of the runners.

Allison was still shaken. Her legs had given out completely, and she was huddling against the wall with her arms around her knees, TJ's arm around her shoulders. Looking up, she saw two figures approaching them quickly and gave a little gasp of surprise. TJ looked up, and a glint appeared in his eye. He casually reached into the pouch where he kept his spellcasting beanbags and withdrew a small packet, unsurprised to find that it wasn't, in fact, a beanbag. He gave it a quick smell and nodded. The wizard uttered a short incantation and tossed the spell reagent lightly into the air. It burst into flames, and when he flicked his hand it flew across the distance to the approaching figures. The ball of fire struck the man on the left and exploded brightly, momentarily blinding both Allison and TJ. When their vision cleared, there was nothing left of either of the brigands, save some burned clothing and the smell of cooked meat.

TJ smiled. "That felt *awesome*!"

"Oh yeah? Well, that was my brother," came a deep voice from their left. One of the bandits had been hiding in the building and stepped toward them, brandishing a wicked-looking dagger.

TJ fumbled desperately with his pouch as he tried to withdraw the reagents needed for another spell. The man grinned wolfishly as he closed the distance between them in two steps. "Tell me how awesome *this* feels," he growled, and thrust his dagger into TJ's chest. The robe provided no protection whatsoever and the blade slid in between two ribs, puncturing a lung. TJ gave a cry of pain and slumped over, the dagger protruding from his chest. His breath grew raspy and he coughed twice, blood and saliva dribbling from between his lips.

Allison stared in horror as her best friend collapsed by her side. She looked up at the man who had stabbed him, fury in her eyes. He met her gaze casually and reached to his belt to draw another dagger. "Well, aren't you a pretty one? I might find a use or two for you," he said, leering. "But first, let's put an end to this one, OK?" He bent over with the new dagger in his hand, ready to slit TJ's throat.

"No!" Allison shouted, and thrust her arms forward, palms outstretched. A surge of power welled up within her, and the next thing she knew, the man was writhing on the ground, clutching his chest in pain. She scrambled up and reached for her mace, which fit snugly in her hand. *"No!"* she shouted again, swinging the weapon with all her strength and bringing it down on his torso. The sound of ribs cracking filled the air, and the man's arms flailed once. She brought the mace down a second time into his face, crushing his nose and cheekbones and putting an end to him once and for all.

Allison paused to look at the body of the fallen bandit, and then she turned to TJ. His breathing was shallow, and the color had drained from his face. His robes were soaked with his own blood and were getting wetter even as she watched. She crouched down and cradled his limp body against her chest, sliding the blade out and casting it aside. Tears fell from her eyes and mingled with the blood leaking from his body. She closed her eyes and sobbed, wishing that things were back to normal—wishing that her best friend was happy and healthy again.

And then she felt a tingling in her body that spread down through her arms and into the palms of her hands. TJ's body heated up. His arms and legs began to twitch, and as the tingling increased, so did his twitches. With a loud gasp he sat bolt upright, chest heaving.

"Wha? Huh? Wha?" His eyes darted around anxiously. When they met Allison's, a great smile stretched across his face. "You. You saved my life. Everything was dark. And it hurt. So much. And then I felt you come into me. I felt your strength, and I felt the pain in my side lessen, and then disappear." He reached down to his blood-soaked robe and gently spread apart the hole where the dagger had gone through. Beneath the cloth was the barest hint of a scar. "You saved me, Allie." He wrapped his arms around her and sobbed into her shoulder. Then TJ looked at her face and saw the lines of concern and exhaustion. The freckles and her eyes. He had never noticed how blue they were. How clear they were.

Stu approached slowly, then cleared his throat. He pointed back outside the encampment. It took them a few moments to realize what he was getting at.

"Simon!" they both shouted at once, then scrambled up from the ground, trying to keep from entangling themselves in each other's legs. TJ's body was still reeling from the damage and the subsequent healing, so Allison sped away from him and around the curve of the wall. When he came up next to where she was standing over Simon, he found her just staring at their friend.

"Aren't you going to fix him?" TJ asked frantically, shaking her by the shoulder. "Why don't you do the same thing you did to me? You should still have plenty of spells left. Your ring alone gave you an extra five! Why aren't you doing anything?"

"It's too late, TJ. He's gone."

Panic crept into his voice. "What do you mean he's gone? Have you checked his pulse? What is that thing we learned in that CPR class? Air passage something?" He bent down to feel for a pulse and put his cheek in front of Simon's slightly open mouth. He almost shouted, "Do something, Allie!"

"No, TJ, there's nothing I can do. It's too late."

He looked back at her. "There must be something we can try! How can you be sure?"

At this, Allison tensed up and shouted, "Because I know, TJ! *I know.* All I had to do was look at him, and I *knew*. I guess that's part of me now. He's dead. And those others by the gate are dead. And I don't hear Jimmy shouting anymore, so I imagine the other bandits are dead too." Her voice softened a bit. "It's part of me, just like that ball of fire you threw is a part of you." She gave a small smile. "Guess it's a good thing you let me choose that smite after all, isn't it?"

TJ stood, giving her arm a slight squeeze.

The three turned and reentered the compound. Stu looked around warily, an arrow nocked and his bow drawn. TJ and Allison, on the other hand, just trudged in, not particularly interested in what there was to see. A figure stepped out from around a corner, and Stu readied to release.

"Whoa there, tiger," called Jimmy. "It's just me. I don't think there's anyone left in here to shoot. After I chased down those other two, I got cornered by a couple more, but well, here I am, so I guess you know what happened." He ran an arm across his forehead and let out a whoosh of air. "You know what? I'm hungry. I wonder what sort of grub they've got here. I hope they knocked over somewhere better than that little village back there."

"Are we sure we got them all?" asked Stu.

Jimmy shrugged. "I got five. What about you?"

Stu replied, "Four for me, including the one in the forest."

Allison chimed in, "Two for me and two for TJ."

"Huh. That makes thirteen. So much for that great intelligence we got. At least the directions were good. Assuming these were the right guys, of course." Jimmy paused and looked around nervously. "Whoa. Wouldn't it stink if we just did this to a bunch of random people? Maybe we should find Chuck and get out of here. I wonder where the little guy's gotten off to."

TJ sighed. "Well, this isn't really the sort of place where we have to worry about the police coming and arresting us, particularly given what those townsfolk had to say about things. Not that I'm saying we ought to make this our new home or anything, but let's not get panicky."

That last statement just hung there as the friends chewed over it.

Allison asked quietly, "*Is* this our new home or anything?"
No one spoke.

CHAPTER 7

"Hey, guys, look at what I found!" Chuck's voice spurred them all out of their reverie. He was holding a small pouch in each hand, and when he shook them they jingled. "There's a couple more of these little bags in that building right over there." He nodded to the side. "Looks like these folks have been doing a pretty brisk business. It's almost all gold, with just a little silver." He stopped in his tracks. "What's wrong? You don't look so good."

Four sets of eyes glared at him, and he suddenly realized that someone was missing. "Um, where's Simon?" It didn't take long for him to understand. "Oh. Crap." He looked at the bags in his hands. "These aren't so important now, are they?"

"No, not really." Allison's voice was hollow.

"K. Well, they're there, when we eventually get around to them." He tossed them to the side—though not too far away—and hunkered down on the ground. He joined them in their silence, though his eyes did keep sliding back to where the small bags of gold lay. "So we got 'em all, right? There aren't any others wandering around?"

Jimmy replied, "Nope, unless they're hiding under a bed, there's no one left in here. Though we probably ought to have someone at the gate in case there was another hunter out and about. Don't think we want to have someone catching us unawares." He raised an eyebrow at Stu, who nodded once and took up a position at the gate.

TJ looked over at Chuck. "So what happened to you? One moment you were right beside us, and the next moment it was just me and Allie."

Chuck looked nervous. "Oh, well, you know. I was keeping an eye on our flanks and stuff. Checking the buildings for anyone who might be hiding and getting ready to jump us. Luckily, I didn't find anyone."

"You ditched us, is what you're saying."

"I didn't ditch you! Not really. I was just making sure I had sufficient cover for the battle. I was more than ready, but there wasn't anyone for me to fight. And then when I heard all the noise die down, and heard you folks talking, I knew we were safe and started to poke around."

"You weaselly little bastard." Allison's voice was laced with venom. "One of our friends is dead outside, and we very nearly lost another one"—reflexively she reached out and laid a hand on TJ—"and all you could think to do was find a place to hide and load up on treasure. I can't believe you."

Chuck shrugged, and his eyes darted back and forth between Allison, TJ, and the pouches of gold. "C'mon, you guys. You know I'm not any good in a fight. I can barely hold this thing without stabbing myself. That's not my job—I'm the Bilbo of the group. I'm here to get you in and out safe and sound." Jimmy's face softened into something resembling acceptance—if not agreement—but both TJ and Allison continued to glare at the little man until he was forced to break eye contact.

"That's not my job either, Jimmy," countered Allison. "But I didn't run. I did what I had to do to keep us alive, unlike you."

"OK, fine," Chuck conceded. "Well, I'll be over there trying to see if there's anything else we can use." He trudged away and let himself through a door into one of the camp's small buildings.

When he was out of earshot, Jimmy said softly, "He's right, you know. It's better that he did. He'd probably just end up getting himself killed in this sort of situation, and we don't have anyone else with the same skills if he did. This wasn't that stupid wolf-man attack back in the woods. This is the real deal." He paused. "And it's not like he could have done anything about Simon anyway. I don't know if there's anything that *any* of us could have done about Simon. That arrow hit him pretty much in the worst place possible. I don't think he felt much."

Allison sighed loudly. "Maybe you're right. But I still wonder. What if I had known then what I know now? Could *I* have done something?"

"Well, I don't know the answer to that," Jimmy replied. "But the truth is, what's done is done, and we can't go back and change it. We should worry about what the future holds. And whether we like it or not, *our* future isn't the one we were expecting it to be this morning."

"Yeah, I guess you're right," said TJ. "But then, you weren't nearly stabbed to death just now. Looks like you came through pretty well unscathed. Maybe I should have taken your lead and put some points into my combat skills back in the real world. Because it looks like they apply here, wherever we are. I can still feel that knife sliding into me." He gave an involuntary shudder. "Maybe you can show me a few tricks I can use to keep myself alive in the future, Jimmy?"

"You bet. And, well, I'm really sorry about your getting stabbed like that. I guess I should have known better than to go charging off, leaving you squishy ones unprotected. I don't know what came over me. It just felt . . . right. Like I had been training my entire life for this one moment, and there it was, and I ran into action. And those bandits we were fighting? I know it didn't seem like it to you, 'cause you got stabbed and all, but to me they were nothing. It felt as if they were acting in slow motion as I moved through them and cut them down. I guess all those weekends of gaining experience, and increasing my ranks and my ability scores, really meant more than just little cards and stats and stuff. We're the real deal: I'm Conan, or Aragorn, or both of them and then some all wrapped up into one. My sword feels alive in my hand, and the armor I'm wearing is weightless."

Stu spoke softly, and yet everyone jumped. He had been so quiet that they'd all forgotten he was there. "I know what you mean, Jimmy. If you're Aragorn, I'm Legolas. You know, I've never picked up a real bow and arrow in my life. Why would I have? And what would I have shot at? I live in the suburbs. But when I saw that guy in the woods, I knew I had to hit him. And when I reached down to grab an arrow from my quiver, my fingers found one instantly. And I placed it in my string and drew back and let it go as if I'd been doing it all my life. You didn't see where I hit him. It was in his throat. And that's because that's where I aimed. If I had aimed at his arm I would have hit him in his arm, and if I had aimed at his leg I would have hit him in the leg. And if I had been aiming to miss him, I could have grazed his ear with my arrow as it flew past.

"And I could do it again. I know I could, as simple as breathing. That's the amazing thing. And you know how I've got that ability to hit something behind a shrub or something, like I did with that wolf man earlier today, but can only do it twice a day? That's not what I did just now. I can feel it. Hitting that guy in the throat is just what I do. And I do it well."

Jimmy nodded. "Exactly. Like that was what you were meant to do."

Stu gave a quick look over his shoulder and back through the gate, but then looked back at Allison and TJ. "What about you two? What do you feel?"

Allison shrugged and said, "Well, you already heard half of it out by Simon's body. I can sense things like that now. As for the other half, well, I don't know what to say. When I reached out and struck the guy who stabbed TJ, it was like I was channeling all my hatred into a little beam, like a laser, and focusing it on one person. And the healing, it was the complete opposite. All of my compassion, all of my caring, all of my will was focused on making him better. At the time, I was just making a fairy-tale wish over and over. But in retrospect, it was much more than that. I wasn't wishing it to happen. I was willing it to happen.

"And you know what? I should probably be lying next to Simon right now." TJ's face contorted, and he reached out to comfort her. She pushed his hand away gently, then continued, "No, I don't mean that in a guilty 'it should have been me' sort of way. I mean that I got hit by an arrow too, but it seemed to bounce right off me." She raised her hand, and the glint of metal was visible on one of her fingers. "Look what I've got. No more three-by-five note card for me. One honest-to-goodness Ring of Ancient Triumph, sitting here on my finger. Power number two, increasing the effectiveness of my armor rating by something or another. A magic ring just saved my life."

TJ took her hand in his and squinted at it. He swooned momentarily as a rush of memories flowed through him. He closed his eyes and shook his head briefly. "Yup, that's what it is all right. And you know all those details on the card about its backstory and such? That barely scratches the surface of this ring's true history. Names, dates, places; I know them all. And if I were to fill you in on it, we would be talking all night long and into tomorrow."

"So you've got all that lore in your head now? Do you really have room for it all?" Jimmy smirked.

TJ returned the smile. "Yeah, I really do. For instance, that sword you're carrying? I could tell you its full history as well. I bet you didn't even know it has a history, but it does."

"Really? How is that possible? This is just the sword I took when I created my character."

"Think about what you said before. You are a *hero* in this world. Not one of the fifty that showed up at the reserve this morning. But *the* one-of-a-kind hero. *Of course* your weapon is something special. And of course that's the sort of lore that we would have studied back at the academy. Understanding what its powers are, and how those powers were infused into it . . . that's important stuff to know.

"Its original name translates into our tongue as 'Lightning,' though that ancient language has long since fallen out of use. It was crafted at the request of a giant of a man, perhaps seven and a half feet tall and weighing in at three-fiftyish. Think Shaq. But bigger and angrier. So this guy, whose name has been lost, didn't want one of those puny swords that everyone carries around. Oh no. He wanted a bigger sword. He carried it one-handed, and it had a shield that went with it. The shield, unfortunately, was splintered by the axe of a minotaur in some cavern somewhere. That's where he died too, having learned too late that while a sword of that size is great when fighting out in the open, it's not so helpful in tight quarters. Anyway, he was something of a lumbering beast, and the sword granted him magical agility. That explains part of why you move so much faster than others. It was also infused with magic as the edges were ground and as the blade was quenched and tempered. This resulted in a razor-sharpness that is unmatched by anything else known to man. Can you remember sharpening it?"

Jimmy scrunched his forehead and then said, "No. I can't really say that I do."

"That's because it doesn't need it. It will never lose its edge. That's part of its magic."

"Sweet."

"Yeah. I don't suppose you know where you found it, do you?"

Jimmy thought for a few moments. "Well, part of me says no, I don't. I just wanted to carry a big honkin' sword when I made up my character, and there it was. But . . ." He trailed off. "But yeah. I do remember where I found it. It was some years ago. I was exploring a cave down south, and I stumbled upon it in a pile of rubbish in some room. I liked the way it looked, so I picked it up and took it with me. And I've been using it ever since.

"But . . . whoa. Where did that memory come from? I can actually remember the smell of those caverns, and the taste of the water that flowed in an underground river. How is that possible?"

TJ shrugged. "The same way it's possible that I know the history of most of the major magical artifacts in this world. We have become our characters. Tell me, how well do you remember high school? Or driving your truck? Or precalculus?"

"Well, the fact that I can't remember any math isn't a shock. Precalc wasn't really my thing. But yeah, I know what you mean. Those memories aren't fading away, per se. They're just becoming less vivid. And new memories are taking their place. Like the fact that I met you at a tavern down in Highpass several years ago, and we have rarely separated since. Or that *you*"—he looked at Allison—"are my buddy's kid sister. Just like we talked about before the game started. I just ran into him . . . last month was it, just before you were scheduled to leave the temple. That's when he told me he couldn't make the trip and asked me to pick you up and keep you safe while he was off on an adventure of his own. If we ever see him again, he's going to be quite surprised when he sees how I bungled that job."

TJ smiled. "I can't wait to hear that conversation. We'll need to make sure that we live long enough to see it. I, for one, remember being recognized as a prodigy early, and being packed off to study with the magicians at the Tower. Years of books before I was given permission to learn even the most rudimentary of spells. Seeing my colleagues struggle and fail at understanding what seemed second nature to me. I rose quickly, and graduated quickly, and went to make my way in the world. And never a second thought about any of it, because of that rush you get when the magic pours through you. It's like crack, I tell you. Or heroin."

Allison shook her head. "That's totally bizarre. I don't have any memories like that. I don't remember learning to use my power, or having an older brother. I mean, I'm an only child!"

The boys exchanged looks and TJ offered, "Well, maybe you don't have any memories because you're such a newbie. We've all had years of adventures, not to mention imagined exploits and a good bit of backstory we've used to fill in the rest of our characters' histories. I guess that since yesterday was the first time you even thought about playing, and you only got your character this morning, you're more of an open book." He shrugged. "Maybe it will fill in over time. Your guess is as good as mine."

They sat in silence for a few minutes until Chuck's voice floated in from around a corner. "I don't suppose you'd like to hear what I have to say, would you?"

TJ and Allison shot each other a glance.

"Sure, what do you have to say, Chuckles?" TJ said, trying to make up for their earlier harshness.

"Well, like you were saying, I've got all this stuff floating through my head that I've never even thought about before. Like, I look over at the wall over there, and I see the places where I would need to put my fingers and feet if I wanted to climb up. And it looks plenty easy. And you know those pouches of gold I found earlier? I didn't really even have to look for them. I walked into one of those buildings and my eyes just found them. They were hidden, but I just *knew* where I should look to find them. I look at the locks on these doors and it makes me laugh. I could open up most of them with a small twig, and one with just my fingers, believe it or not."

His voice dropped a little. "And I have those memories. Memories that I know aren't mine, but at the same time I know they *are* mine. Little snippets of character that I never thought about when I made up this character for a weekend of gaming. Like how I grew up alone on the streets of Westmarch and was taken in by the guild there. They turned me into the finest pickpocket, lockpick, and cat burglar of our generation, and I spent years breaking into houses and robbing people blind. And even though they had me committing crimes my entire youth, all I can feel for them is gratitude. The alternative would have been being rounded up and pressed into service, or being abducted by those with less than savory tastes.

"And I remember the beatings I received by those who thought they were better than me and thought they deserved more respect, more prestige. They were always careful to avoid damaging my fingers—the master would have had them killed for risking my earning potential—but the beatings were horrible. That was what eventually drove me away from the Westmarch and into the company of mercenaries." He waved his hand at his companions. "I tried to fight back from time to time, but it was never any good." His shoulders drooped. "And you wonder why I ran and hid when things went south. I'm not a fighter. I've never been a fighter. But what I *am* is a survivor."

Silence fell over the group as each one digested what they had heard, and what they were learning about themselves as their minds absorbed new memories.

"Well, I don't know about any of you," Jimmy finally said, "but I'm still hungry."

CHAPTER 8

Both TJ and Allison realized they were ravenous as well. The energy involved in the healing—on both sides—seemed to have taken a toll on their bodies. No one in the group had bothered to pack food in their bags, since the gamers typically returned to the lodge for meals. However, their transition to the game world seemed to have included day-to-day sundries in addition to their armor and weapons; each found a small cache of dried beef in their gear. TJ took a bite of his and chewed. And chewed. And chewed.

"Whoa, this stuff is horrible." He made a face. "Let's see what they've got in their larder."

Chuck pointed over his shoulder with his thumb and said, "It's that hut just over there. The one with the low ceiling. They've got quite a spread, from what I was able to see. Looks like they've been roving all over the place, stealing from just about everyone nearby. I'd say they have enough food set aside for several weeks for the lot of 'em. Some cheese. Some pepperoni-looking things. Kinda reminds me of the Pepperidge Farm store at Christmastime." He tittered. "Nothing says merry Christmas like a yard o' beef, huh?"

Allison laughed. "Yard o' beef I could take or leave. That cheese sounds really good, though. Lead the way, little man."

No one had noticed it before, but as he led them to the larder, it became clear that Chuck was the smallest of the group. He wasn't hobbit small, or dwarf small, but he definitely fit the stereotype of a cutpurse or a burglar sneaking in and out of tight spaces. He was light on his feet, graceful even, and he looked like he was ready to dodge an attack from any direction at any time, even though they all knew the camp was empty. Similarly, Jimmy appeared to have grown several inches in both height and breadth since the morning.

The larder was everything he described, and more. Meats and cheeses hung from pegs along the walls, and casks of flour, beans, and other dry goods were stacked in rows. At the back, a trapdoor led to a root cellar filled with potatoes and onions. A soft clucking coming through the wall suggested that there was a chicken coop somewhere nearby as well.

"As odd as this sounds," said Jimmy, "I have no interest in killing a chicken. Those five people I sliced open? No problem. But a poor defenseless chicken? I don't think I could do it."

"You just don't want to have to pluck the thing, lazy," joked TJ.

Jimmy grinned back at his friend. "Well, yeah, there's that too."

They rummaged through the provisions, gathering a little of this and a little of that, then returned to the sunlight to sit and chew. While they all would have preferred a nice hot stew cooked in the compound's fire pit, they knew there were other things to deal with first. So after they had sated their hunger, the five stood up.

"Well, what do you think we should do first?" TJ asked.

Allison replied, "Let's get these brutes out of sight. We can drag them out into the woods and let the wolves eat them. That's the best they deserve." The others knew she was just delaying the inevitable, not yet wanting to face the reality of Simon's death. No one called her on it.

The others nodded, and Chuck piped in, "Wait a sec, lemme see if they've got anything of value on 'em first. Always search the bodies!" Noticing the look of distaste on Allison's face, he added, "Look, Allison. I know you're a newbie and all, but you're going to have to get used to this. We are adventurers, and being an adventurer costs a lot of coin. Unless you want to retire in some village somewhere and be a farmer's wife, you're going to have to accept that we'll be pulling stuff off the bodies.

"Besides, if there's anything of value on them, what's the point in leaving it out in the woods for the wolves to chew on? Where do you think they got all that stuff? If you want, we can do the Robin Hood thing and give to the poor, but just letting it all rot is stupid."

"OK, fine," she sighed. "I guess you're right. I don't have to like it, though."

With a shrug, Chuck began to rummage through the clothing of each of the bodies, and examined their fingers and ears for any jewelry. He didn't think it likely, but there was always a possibility that a fallen foe carried an item of magical nature. The world wasn't lousy with magic rings and amulets and the like, but they weren't as scarce as one might think. As Frodo himself had discovered, it was extremely difficult to destroy a magical item, so they began to build up over time as new ones were created. Unfortunately, other than a few small pieces of jewelry and the coin in their pouches, there was nothing for

Chuck to report. The stuff he did find, however, went into a small bag that he agreed would go to the villagers they'd met earlier. They dragged the dead bodies out of the compound and over to the tree line near the body of the archer Stu had shot.

Reluctantly, they then turned to Simon's body, which still lay in the shade of the wall with the arrow sticking out of his chest. The five gathered around him and spent a few minutes in silence.

"We should dig a grave," Stu remarked.

"Yeah," Jimmy replied.

No one moved for several long moments. "I'll go find a shovel or two," said Jimmy.

"I'll come with," Stu offered.

The two trudged into the compound, leaving the other three behind. Not long after, Chuck slipped away, muttering something about the call of nature. Neither TJ nor Allison responded, and perhaps they didn't even notice. The two stood together, looking down at their friend.

"You know, I was really excited to learn that he was going to be here," said Allison. "On some level I thought it meant this wasn't going to be as geeky as I'd imagined. Of course," she added, chuckling, "it was actually every bit as geeky as I imagined. You have to admit that the king's speech was over-the-top melodramatic."

TJ grunted his agreement.

"But anyway, now I feel guilty about that. Not that that makes any sense, I know. It had nothing to do with what I wanted. He was going to come whether I did or not. But I still feel guilty anyway. I feel responsible. And maybe that's the healer in me talking, but I feel like I should have done more. I should have done something. I should have . . ." She choked up as she trailed off.

TJ put his arm around her shoulder but didn't say anything. Nothing he could think to say seemed appropriate.

Jimmy and Stu came back, each carrying a shovel. Allison looked over and sighed. "Give me one of those," she said, and took the one Stu held. She turned and surveyed the area. A portion of the clearing was sprinkled with wildflowers, and that was where she pointed. "He should go there."

The ground was heavy and full of clay once they got through the first layer of topsoil, so it was harder than they expected. Even so, working together and trading off the shovels as their shoulders got tired, they had the hole dug within an hour. With the ground cleared, Stu and Jimmy carried Simon's body over and placed it in the grave. Chuck had come back, and they each took turns shoveling the dirt over him. When the hole was filled, Allison replaced some of the flowers in the dirt. They then stood quietly, listening to the wind rustling through the leaves and birds chirping.

"It's peaceful. I guess that's appropriate," Chuck murmured.

Allison nodded, then turned and walked to the compound without a backward glance. The others all followed, one by one, until Simon was left alone. And there he remained.

CHAPTER 9

By the time they finished laying Simon to rest, the sun had begun to set, turning their shadows into black giants. While no one was particularly happy with the idea of staying the night at the brigands' camp, by consensus it was decided that doing so was preferable to sleeping out in the woods in unfamiliar territory. Stu was confident he could find them a place to set up camp that would be protected from the elements and wild animals, but that hardly made sense when they had a solid wall surrounding them.

A number of cooking pots were stacked neatly in a corner of the larder building. A casual inspection indicated that they were well scrubbed and free of grime. It appeared that even outlaws took cleanliness seriously, at least when it had a potential effect on their health. TJ took a medium-sized one from the stack and filled it with chunks of the meat, as well as some potatoes and onions from the root cellar. A nearby barrel was discovered to be filled with water, collected from a series of gutters attached to the roof of one of the buildings. He filled the pot the rest of the way with the water and lugged it over to the fire pit, where Stu had already coaxed a flame to life. They banked the coals and set the pot in the middle of them. Soon the smell of stew filled the air and set the group's stomachs rumbling.

Darkness fell as the food finished cooking, and the firelight danced in the crisp air. They ladled their meal into some wooden bowls and ate it with hard bread taken from the larder.

Jimmy broke the silence by asking, "So now what?"

"Now what, what?" TJ replied.

"Now what do we do? Somehow we got here, and we have taken on the skills and memories of the made-up characters we were playing this morning. What do we do now? Just go on living like this? I'll say it's pretty cool to have these abilities and stuff. I'll also say that Simon was a friend of mine, and that whole getting shot and killed violently thing wasn't really in my long-term plans. I was planning on going to college and becoming an accountant. Not glamorous, but a good living. I'd kind of like to go back home, if you know what I mean."

Allison snorted. "You're telling me. I wasn't even going to come to this thing until TJ started harassing me. I kind of like the idea of indoor plumbing and not getting cholera and stuff. Though I guess if someone got cholera I would probably be able to cure them . . . but that's not the point. How are we going to get back home?"

The question hung there until TJ spoke. His voice carried a sense of authority that hadn't been there before, suggesting that it wasn't him that was speaking as much as Galphalon. "Well, we crossed over into this world sometime between the wolf men and the village. If you recall, they seemed confused by our use of game references, such as Simon's diplomacy score. And if we had really been thinking about it, we would have realized that there were just too many NPCs at that encounter. Where would they have gotten those kids to play in the dirt?

"When specifically it happened, who knows? So I guess we have two choices. One would be to go back down the path in case there was something physical that we passed through, or near, that made all this happen." He gestured to the world around them with his hands. "Something makes me think that's probably not the answer. If it was simply a portal we walked through, the other groups would almost certainly have been transported here as well, and there was at least one group ahead of us that the villagers would have seen. They didn't mention anything, so I assume that means it wasn't something physical.

"The other option would be to continue on and try to figure out the *reason* we were brought here." He spoke the word *reason* in a reverent tone. "Assuming we were, the only choice we have is to carry on and see where we find ourselves on the other end of this. The trick will be determining what that reason actually is. Is it the same story we were given by our 'king'? Or is it something else completely?

"If you ask my opinion, I think that for good or ill we can only go forward. Maybe we will find our way back home, and maybe we won't. Just sitting around here and doing nothing, however, doesn't seem to be an option."

Stu suggested, "Well, we *could* just sit around here and do nothing. This is the sort of place where someone could live, with a bit of work tilling up some fields. It's not like this would be a hard place to defend either." At the looks he received from Allison and Jimmy, he raised his hands in defense. "I'm not suggesting that we actually do that, but it's an option."

TJ shook his head. "No. Honestly, I don't think it is. Have you noticed how we all have been changing? We saw how

Jimmy reacted when the battle started. And Chuck." He shot a quick glance at his friend, who grinned sheepishly. "And tell me, Stu. When you shot that guy earlier, how did it feel to you? I'm willing to bet it didn't feel like anything. Certainly not what it should have felt for a teenager to kill another human being. I know that because I incinerated two of them, and the only thing I felt was exhilaration. That's not normal. At least not for people who aren't psychopaths.

"We are changing. We've gained the skills of our characters, but as we saw with Chuck, we've also gained our characters' memories. Stu, what you told us about the greybeard moss earlier. About spending all that time in these woods. Whose memory was that? Was it yours, or your character's? Are you sure you even know the difference anymore? I'm not so sure that I do. Sure, we could stay here, but eventually the desires that originally drove our characters to become adventurers will become too strong to suppress, and we'll be out fighting monsters and rescuing damsels and recovering lost relics. We probably won't lose ourselves, but the selves we are going to become won't be satisfied living as peasant farmers."

"There *is* a third possibility," Allison chimed in. Eight eyes turned her way. "Let's say for a moment that the story we were told is true. That wizard guy has gotten super powerful and is trying to conquer the world, and the world isn't necessarily going to give up easily. Maybe we are just innocent bystanders, and because of some random piece of magic being flung around here, we got sucked in by mistake. No *reason* to it. It just sort of happened. Then what?"

TJ smiled. "I'd decided not to bring that up for the sake of morale. Yes, that's a possibility. And if that's what happened, then perhaps we're out of luck. We're never going home, and we're going to live out the rest of our lives as the great adventurers we were playing. If we're lucky, those lives will be relatively long. If we're not, well, then perhaps the bards will sing of us after we pass.

"But the reality is that we don't know what really happened. Maybe we're here for a *reason*, and maybe we're here just by accident. What does that do to our decision process? A couple years ago, I read Ian Fleming's James Bond series. One thing stuck with me, other than the fact that Fleming was an atrocious bigot. Bond was playing bridge—the card game, you know?—against some nemesis at a gentlemen's club, and for some reason he was stuck with a really high bid to make." His friends' looks had gone blank at the mention of bridge. "Just humor me. He had a very small shot at winning."

They nodded.

"Anyway, this is what he said. If there is only one way to win, and it is dependent on something that is uncertain—in this case who had a particular card in their hand—the only thing you can do is play as if you know for a fact that it is true. Maybe it's not. Maybe winning was never an option. But if it turns out you were right, you may end up bucking the odds after all."

Jimmy smirked. "So what you're saying is that whether we actually have a chance at getting out of here is irrelevant. We carry on and hope that we can get this sorted out and get ourselves back home. Either we will or we won't, but if we start out by assuming we can't, we definitely won't."

"Yeah, pretty much."

"Huh. Good point."

The group stewed over TJ's assessment as they ate their meal. No one really felt like talking after everything they'd been through that day. After TJ had finished his second helping, he tossed the bowl into the fire. When the others looked at him, he said, "I dunno. Just sort of feels like the right thing to do. One last protest against it all."

Four other bowls followed TJ's into the fire, and the friends watched them be consumed by the flames. The bowls hissed briefly as the moisture sizzled out of them, and then the only sound was the crackling of the wood as it burned.

After a time, Chuck said, "I guess we could torch the whole place."

The group exchanged looks as they considered the suggestion.

At last Jimmy said, "No, I don't think that's the right thing to do. There is a lot here that people could use." He gestured around them. "People could even live here. It is defensible, and the clearing has enough room for someone to plant a large garden. We already saw that there's game nearby. Those poor bastards in the woods . . . they could make a better life here."

The others nodded at the suggestion, and then everyone retreated into their own thoughts. They were still sitting in silence when the moon rose and their eyes began to get heavy. The fire dimmed and they all prepared their bedrolls. The brigands had bunkhouses, but no one wanted to sleep in them, partly on principle and partly because they were all infested with bugs. Newfound instincts urged them to set a watch, and they divvied up the shifts, though it turned out to be unnecessary as the night passed uneventfully. In retrospect, it made sense that they would sleep undisturbed. These were the local bad guys—who in their right mind would try to attack them? The local peasantry was vastly outmatched, and if what Claude had said was true, the local soldiery was as likely as not to just exchange pleasantries and pass on by.

The next morning as they were preparing to leave, Chuck handed each of them a pouch that jingled when shaken. He said, "I know you may not care now, but we really do need to have money as we proceed. There are several more pouches with a similar amount that we can give to whomever we feel deserves it. If you ask me, we should keep it for ourselves, but I suspect you're not going to ask me, so whoever wants to hold on to them is welcome to. There's enough coin in each of these bags to make a huge difference in some folks' lives." He gestured to a small pile by the gate. "They're over there."

Allison gathered four others, which she tucked into one of the satchels she had found in the storeroom. The others had all taken bags as well, and they loaded up on provisions. They wanted to take at least several days' worth with them.

With one final glance toward Simon's grave, the group headed back into the woods, resuming their marching order from the prior day. Stu, in the lead, had become almost catlike in his ability to choose his steps so as to make no noise whatsoever. The others had also gained more skill, but he was clearly in his element. Allison and TJ occasionally stepped on a twig or a dry leaf, making a slight crunching sound, and each time it happened, everyone grimaced. Still, someone would have to have been actively listening to hear their passage.

The group moved more quickly south than it had north the day before. They each felt more comfortable with their skills and reasoned that if those brigands were the local toughs, there was unlikely to be anything of significant danger in the area. Given how easily they had bested them, the group felt up to a new challenge. It was well before lunch when they first began to smell the smoke from the village's cook fires.

They came out of the woods just down the path from the town and retraced their steps from the previous day. The children were playing outside as before, though this time they didn't panic and run. Rather, the one called Fin looked up calmly and called over his shoulder. "Hey, Paw! Them soldiers are back again." Then he returned to his play.

Claude came running from around the corner of the house, carrying his pitchfork. He pulled up short and looked them over. "So you're back now, milady?" He left the statement floating, waiting for her response.

"Indeed we are, Claude. We have good news, and sad news. The good news is that the brigands won't be bothering you anymore. We came across their encampment yesterday, just as your boy said we would. We killed them all, as well as the one who had returned from hunting. Unless they sent out more than one in search of food, there are none left. Their encampment is empty, and if you and your people want to move in, you may find it more to your liking than staying here." She gestured to the ramshackle buildings along the path. "It has a stout fence around it, and while it might be tight quarters, there would be enough room for all of you. There is even space for you to plant some small crops, and it appears game is plentiful.

"Oh, and there is this." She reached into her satchel and tossed the man one of the pouches of gold. "It is yours now."

Whether due to the magical ring on her finger or something else, the look on Claude's face was nothing short of awe. "Can what you say really be true?" he asked. He opened the thong on the pouch and looked inside, then poured a couple of the coins out into his hand, where the gold shimmered even in the dappled forest light.

Allison nodded. "It is. What you do with your lives now is up to you. But at least you have one less thing to worry about. And should you decide to move your village, perhaps even fewer. There are weapons there too. A few bows, and the swords that the brigands wielded. If the soldiers harass you as you claim, they may be less willing to do so if you can spill their blood from behind a wall. I assume some of you know how to use a bow?"

He nodded back at her. "Yes, milady. There's me, of course, and a couple others who have hunted in their time and still have a strong enough back to draw a bow."

"Then I suggest you make the most of this situation. Over time you can extend the clearing and perhaps create larger fields for crops. We are going on our way now. We wish you the brightest of futures."

"Th-th-thank you, milady," he stuttered.

Her friends watched the exchange in amazement, impressed at how Allison had grown into the role of noblewoman priestess. When she set off down the road through the village, they naturally fell into step behind her. Claude stretched out a hand and grabbed at Allison's sleeve as she passed. She stopped and looked at him with a raised eyebrow.

"Yes, Claude?"

"What was the bad news you spoke of?" His eyes scanned down the line of adventurers and then back to hers, realizing the answer.

"We lost one of our own. He lies among the flowers in the clearing where he died." Her eyes bore into his with an intensity that made him drop his gaze. "Whatever you and your people choose, make the choice worth his sacrifice." With that, she began walking again. She paused briefly in front of the boy, Fin, to pat him on the head, then continued past the other houses and down the path into the woods.

CHAPTER 10

Without any reason to change direction, the group continued down the path, putting Claude's little village behind them. They briefly discussed moving back into the woods, as they had after the first ambush, but concluded that the Obligatory Thug Attack they experienced earlier was merely standard gaming fare, and it probably didn't reflect the real dangers of the road. The path wasn't particularly well trodden, and if someone was looking to cause mischief, the village they had just passed through would be a much surer target than hoping for random passersby. Further, Stu's senses had increased significantly. He claimed there was virtually no chance that he could be taken off guard like that again. Considering how they all manifested their own character's powers, no one doubted his claim.

Morning passed into afternoon, but as the friends got hungry they munched on some of the food from the brigand camp rather than stop their march. There was a sense of urgency now that they had decided to pursue the adventure to the end. Every so often Chuck would make a whiney noise, but it seemed to be more a function of his newfound personality and less one of actual fatigue. When evening began to fall, they slowed their pace and Stu trotted off, crisscrossing the path, looking for a suitable place to camp. It wasn't long before his sharp eyes spotted one, and the group hunkered down.

With flint and steel he had commandeered from the fort, Stu quickly set sparks flying into a pile of tinder. Soon there was a small blaze going, and with branches that the others had brought back to the site, it quickly grew into a respectable campfire. As they sat around the fire, again they ate the dried meat and cheese from their packs.

Between bites, Jimmy said, "You know, I'm not the complaining type or anything, but this stuff was OK while we were walking. I don't think I can live on it indefinitely."

TJ sighed. "Yeah, I agree. These travel rations are good in a pinch, but who knows how long we'll be walking on this path looking for a clue as to what's going to happen next. I don't think we should count on this being a short-term trek. We're going to need to start keeping an open eye for game as we go."

Stu shrugged. "I've seen traces of all sorts of stuff as we've been walking. There's plenty to eat, but hunting is time-consuming, and I wasn't sure if we wanted to slow down for me to restock. Rabbits and birds are easy enough to catch, but they're tricky to find as we march. Deer I can find without any trouble, but cleaning them takes a little more work."

Allison added, "We're not going to be able to eat a whole deer in one meal, are we? How are we going to carry the extra meat?"

"Well, some of it we can smoke overnight while we're sleeping, and that will replenish what we've eaten from our packs already. The rest"—he shrugged again—"we can just leave behind."

"Isn't that kind of wasteful? I thought I read that the Native Americans found a use for every bit of the animals they killed."

At that, the archer smiled. "The part that's growing in me respects your concern. As for the Native Americans, they had the benefits of camping in one place for a week or more at a time, as well as being a much larger group. If they killed a deer it might feed the tribe for a day or two tops. We don't have the luxury of either their numbers or their leisure. I can guarantee that it won't go to waste, however. I've seen wolf tracks crossing the path from time to time. This will just be one less deer they have to run down and kill themselves. It won't upset the environment at all."

"OK, I'll take your word for it. This isn't exactly my area of expertise."

Stu abruptly stood up and said, "Looks like we've got a bit of light yet. Let me go see what I can find out there." The others watched him leave the circle, but once he was past the first line of trees, he blended in with the foliage and they lost sight of him completely.

Chuck said, "Now *that* is talent." Coming from a born pickpocket, that was high praise indeed.

When he was sure Stu was out of earshot, TJ said, "He hasn't been talking much. I hope he's not going to snap or anything. He may be our best hope of staying alive until we find civilization."

Jimmy nodded thoughtfully, and Allison said, "Nah, he's always been like that. His home life is, well, *chaotic* would be a good word. His two sisters chatter almost nonstop at the dance studio, even when Madame yells at them. And his brothers split time between basketball and Xbox. He's kinda the odd guy out. It doesn't surprise me that he likes the quiet of the forest. It's probably the only quiet he gets."

Crickets began to chirp as the sun disappeared. The friends continued to add pieces of wood to the fire as it dimmed, but they were all careful to avoid looking directly into it. The bright firelight would ruin their night vision, which would put them at a severe disadvantage if they were attacked.

"So here we are, out in the middle of nowhere," Jimmy said, and then fell silent.

"And?" asked Allison.

"And nothing really, I guess. I was just thinking aloud. Here we are out in the middle of nowhere. Now what? I mean, I know what we talked about last night, but I don't know. I just feel dissatisfied with the whole thing. Are we just going to keep walking down the path until something happens? Is that really the extent of our plan?"

"Yeah, pretty much," replied TJ.

Allison snorted and the others quickly followed suit.

When Stu returned, silent as a cat, he found the group howling with laughter. "What did I miss? Good joke?"

"No, actually it wasn't," admitted TJ. "But it came out at exactly the right time." The giggling subsided. "We were just talking about what to do next. And I think that our best bet is to continue on. Either something will happen or it won't, and eventually we'll come across a town. If nothing has materialized between now and then, we can reassess, but we certainly can't just sit out here in the woods indefinitely. We have to go *somewhere*."

"Guess so," said Jimmy, but he still sounded unconvinced. "How'd things go out in the woods, Stu? I don't see any deer draped across your shoulder, so I guess it was a bust?"

Stu squatted next to the fire and poked it with a stick. He seemed unconcerned about the fire's effects on his pupils. "It wasn't a bust, exactly. I didn't come back with anything, though, if that's what you're asking. I set some snares in some likely places, and when the bunnies come out tonight, perhaps a few won't find their way back home. With luck we'll have some nice rabbit tomorrow. Seeing as we don't really have a destination, we don't have a timetable either. There won't be any harm done if we have a nice leisurely breakfast."

TJ nodded. "That's fair, though we probably shouldn't make a habit out of it. If we've got to go stop some evil wizard from wreaking havoc on the people of the West, we ought to try to be snappy about it. But for tomorrow, I'm all about a nice brace of rabbits."

Before they bedded down for the night, both Stu and TJ took some precautions to help keep the campsite safe. TJ realized that his character had, on a whim long ago, learned a few spells that were not directly related to combat but that he thought he might need some day. One was a sentry spell that would alert the caster if any creatures larger than a fox came within a fifty-foot radius. The gaming system was developed by a national organization and presumed people would be sleeping out in the woods, so a spell like that would save the caster and his friends from having to set sentries all night long. Their own group, however, always returned to the lodge and bedded down there for the night under its safe and secure roof, so he had never actually used it. He was grateful for it now.

Stu took a more mundane approach to campsite security. He strung a thin twine—invisible unless you were looking for it—between the trunks of trees that surrounded their campsite. Hanging from the twine were small bells that would ring if the twine was touched. His body had long since been trained to awaken to the sound of those bells, so he felt comfortable setting them and then going to sleep. The fire would keep away any animals, and any other undesirables would trigger at least one of the two alarm systems.

As the others settled in to sleep, Chuck performed his own bunking-down ritual. Slinging his satchel over his shoulders, he spent a few moments scanning the branches above the camp. Spotting a likely candidate, he approached the tree's trunk and tentatively placed his fingers on the bark. Nodding to himself, he shinnied up the tree in seconds, then straddled the branch he had picked out. A crow gave a squawk of protest at having to share the limb, and he waved his hands to shoo it away. The bird bobbed its head and flitted to a nearby tree. Chuck quickly wrapped a rope around his waist and tied it to both the branch and the trunk. The little man then leaned back against the trunk and closed his eyes. In moments, he was asleep.

"Whatever floats your boat, I guess," Jimmy said, and rolled over. The others followed suit, and soon the only sound was the crackling of the fire and the soft snores of the four on the ground. Chuck's sleep was noiseless.

CHAPTER 11

TJ sat bolt upright in alarm. An air-raid siren was going off somewhere, and he jerked his head around, looking for the source. No matter which direction he turned, he couldn't pinpoint the noise. It was only after several long seconds that he realized the noise was coming from between his two ears. He dismissed the alarm spell with a thought, irritated that it was nondirectional. He could have sworn that it was supposed to indicate which portion of the perimeter had been breached. That was what his instructors had said would happen.

Unless . . .

A light tinkling noise rang out from his left. And his right. Then behind him.

"Wake up!" he shouted, rousing Allison and Jimmy from their bedrolls. Stu, having sprung up at the first jingle, already had an arrow nocked and was scanning for targets. A shape charged in from the left, and the arrow streaked toward it. The figure emitted a muffled grunt and dropped. No sooner had Stu released his string than he'd pulled another from its quiver. Again he drew and fired, this time in the opposite direction. A second whatever-it-was dropped.

A slight fog had blown in. While it did not completely obstruct TJ's view, it made it difficult to pinpoint details. *"Light!"* he shouted, raising his fist into the air. A dazzling brilliance sprouted from it, giving him his first clear look at the area. Allison reached for her helmet and mace; she had been sleeping in her breastplate. Jimmy was also on his feet and had his sword out in front of him, his back to the campfire.

Most disheartening was the number of enemies that had begun to crowd their camp. A quick count showed a dozen or more in just the front row, and movement in the trees behind suggested at least that many in reserve. They were large, hulking brutes, with knotty foreheads and arms that nearly reached the ground. They wore no armor and carried thick wooden clubs as wide as a man's thigh. Despite their lack of sophisticated weapons, they looked plenty formidable.

Jimmy took two steps forward to meet the first rank and cut at them with his giant sword. Cries of pain and rage followed the tip of his blade as trails of red opened up across arms, chests, and abdomens. Unaware or indifferent to his greater reach, they continued to press in on him and received another slice for their troubles. One toppled, and then another. A third staggered toward Jimmy, club raised high, but the berserker pirouetted, his sword a silver streak that severed both arms and head from the creature's torso.

Stu continued to fire arrow after arrow, but it seemed that his first shots had been lucky to drop the creatures. He now found himself having to fire two or more at the same target to get it to fall, and he was running out of both arrows and space to fire. One stepped close, and he spun his bow around like a staff, catching it on the side of the head. The shaft splintered and the creature merely shook its head in confusion before advancing once again. Stu reached down to grab his sword from where it lay next to his bedroll and brought it up just in time to parry a club crashing down at his skull. The shock from the blow sent pain shooting up his arm, nearly causing him to lose his grip. Another of the beasts had stepped up beside his fellow and swung at Stu as well. Again, his blade turned aside the club, but this time his fingers went numb and the hilt dropped from his grasp. The first one's club came crashing down upon his head.

Allison had taken up a protective position in front of TJ, since she had her breastplate for protection and he had only robes. A small voice inside his head wished that game designers would let wizards wear real armor, but he quashed it. Three bolts of energy sprung from his hands, surging toward the attackers directly in front of her and striking them in their hairy torsos. Their targets each staggered back a step or two, but they didn't seem terribly put out by the attack. He sent a second volley toward the beasts, then a third, and it was the last set that brought them down to their knees. While they were dazed, Allison stepped forward and made quick work of them, bashing in their heads one at a time.

"Well, that was the last of those spells," he said. "I hope there aren't many more." As another rank stepped into the light, he sighed and sent a ball of flame toward them, just as he'd done with the brigands at the camp. Unlike the brigands, when the flame struck them and exploded, the creatures did not look particularly worse for wear. One of them, he could swear, actually smiled. "Really?" he said in exasperation. "Immune to fire? *Really?*"

"How bad is it?" Allison asked.

"Really, really bad. I specialize in fire magic. I don't have a whole lot else at my disposal."

"Yeah, that's pretty bad." She gritted her teeth and readied her mace.

Behind them, Jimmy was still holding his own. He had gotten into a rhythm—swing, stab, swing, stab—that kept the monsters at bay. The length of his blade made it impossible for them to get close enough to do damage with their clubs; the ones that tried to sneak into his sword's radius lost limbs, heads, or both. He made a mental note to ask TJ more about the sword's history—if they managed to get out alive. It seemed to have taken on a life of its own. Swing, stab. Swing, stab.

Out of the corner of his eye he saw Stu go down. While the part that was still Jimmy wanted to aid his friend, or at least to avenge him, his warrior instincts told him to keep his back to the fire and his eyes on those in front of him. He knew that as soon as he let his guard down or tried to turn aside, one of them would sneak through his defense and score a hit. It wasn't that he was afraid of a club hit, or two, or three. He could remember taking much more damage than that and laughing it off. But a lucky shot could break a rib or an arm, or catch him on the head and stun him. And that would be all the opportunity needed to take him out. So he continued to swing and stab, occasionally stepping forward and catching one of the creatures off guard.

Behind him, Allison and TJ were hard-pressed. She had no shield to ward off the blows and cursed herself for turning down the one her uncle had offered from the wardrobe department. At the time she had thought it was overkill, too heavy to lug around all weekend. Showed how little she knew. But she did know that it was only a matter of time before her defenses were overwhelmed. While she had quickness on her side, they had reach. She could dodge in and land a blow and duck out of the way of their slow, powerful strokes, but she would eventually fatigue, and they would get lucky. She had already taken several blows to her shoulders that she had somehow managed to shake off. The ring, most likely. But she couldn't help remembering that she had only a single meager point in the mace skill, and basically nothing else to help her survive the melee.

TJ mumbled some words and pulled a dagger shining with a fey glow from his robes. As he stepped forward to slash, the light emanating from the blade seemed to extend at just the right time to score a cut. "This is a bad thing," he said, huffing and puffing in exertion. "I can't remember how many times I've said that if I had to fight melee we were doomed." A club crashed into his weapon hand, sending the dagger clattering to the side.

"Get behind me!" Allison hissed. She reached out with her left hand and grabbed at his robe, trying to pull him back. He let her pull him, partly because he knew he had no business trying to fight these things hand to hand, and partly because she was quite a bit stronger than he was, and he knew he wasn't going to win.

The effort of moving TJ set Allison off balance, so when the next blow came at her, she wasn't able to parry it. The wooden club slid down her mace and caught her on the wrist, eliciting a gasp of pain. She reached out with a smite, which pushed the creature back and stunned it long enough for her to regain her balance and send a small healing surge into her wrist. That turned out to be a mistake. The energy her body used to heal sent her vision swimming, and she didn't see the club coming from her left side. It crashed into her shoulder and she heard her arm snap, the pain driving her to her knees. The last thing she saw was TJ standing over her and shouting, holding her mace awkwardly with two hands. He barely lasted ten seconds.

Jimmy, unaware that the last of his allies had fallen, continued to stay focused on those in front of him and, to a lesser extent, to the sides. As a result of the latter, he was taken unawares by a creature who tackled him from behind. With a whoosh of air from his lungs, he dropped his sword and was pinned to the ground, where he was kicked savagely with steel-lined boots. For once he regretted his ability to withstand damage; unconsciousness didn't come soon enough.

CHAPTER 12

Chuck, up in the tree, was awoken by the sound of TJ rustling around. His body had long since learned to rouse at the slightest sound. While it had caused him quite a few restless nights, it had also saved his life more times than he could count. By the time Stu's bells began to chime, he was fully awake. The first thing he did—the first thing he always did when confronted with danger—was to make himself very, very small. He had found over the years that the smaller he made himself, the less likely his enemies were to spot him. And were they actually to notice him, they'd undoubtedly underestimate him. He preferred the former to the latter, but either worked.

So he scrunched up against the trunk of the tree in which he had been sleeping, putting the thickest portion of the branch he was on between himself and the campsite. A quick look around revealed a branch of similar thickness on the opposite side of the tree, so he darted onto it, quiet as a squirrel. His speed was rewarded—at just that moment a blazing light burst from TJ's upstretched hand. Had Chuck still been sitting on his original branch, anyone looking up would have seen him with no trouble.

Peering around the trunk, he surveyed the scene. If any part of him envisioned playing the savior and jumping from the tree to the aid of his comrades, what he saw put the kibosh on that immediately. Within the ring of trees where his friends had camped were perhaps twenty or so of the behemoth creatures. The kobolds. He knew they were called kobolds. But that in and of itself wasn't so bad. He had memories of Jimmy and TJ taking on similar odds and coming out unscathed. What caused him the most worry were the rows of the creatures lurking just outside the tree line. The twenty beasts in the ring were easily outnumbered by the ones waiting in backup, and it was only a matter of time—and not a very long time at that—before all of his friends went down. He knew that joining the combat would have no effect on the outcome whatsoever.

And so he watched. And waited. When Stu's bow shattered across the kobold's head, Chuck cringed, but Allison seemed to be holding her own, particularly when combined with the magical blasts that TJ shot from his fingers. When TJ threw the ball of flame at the second row, Chuck allowed himself to become slightly hopeful. He had seen the effect of those attacks in the past, most recently at the brigand camp, where he'd been peering from behind a corner. His heart sank, however, when he saw that it hadn't done any good. He knew it was over.

The battle wrapped up quickly, with Jimmy dropping almost immediately after Allison and TJ had been knocked down. Chuck wanted to look away, fearing that his friends were going to become dinner right before his eyes. He forced himself to continue watching, though, as a silent testament to their bravery. One of the beasts bent down to where TJ had fallen on top of Allison and began sniffing. Experimentally, it stuck out a tongue and slid it across Allison's face. It licked its chops, then opened its mouth to take a bite.

Another kobold bounded forward with a howl and cuffed it in the head, sending the hungry one tumbling. It jumped back to its feet and lunged forward, but was cuffed again, harder. The one that Chuck assumed to be the leader growled a challenge, standing over the bodies of the companions and swinging his club menacingly. The growl was returned, though with a more submissive sound, and the loser left the fire ring with a backward glance.

Much to Chuck's surprise, he was not forced to watch his friends be devoured. The leader growled another order, and several of the brutes took out ropes and tightly bound the arms and legs of the adventurers. Each was then thrown over a beast's shoulder, and the attackers melted back into the woods. In less than a minute the normal noises of the forest returned. All that remained of the fight were the monsters that had died in the assault. It appeared that they weren't really interested in burials.

His instincts honed on the rough-and-tumble streets, Chuck counted slowly to one hundred, breathing lightly and remaining stock-still. Only then did he unharness himself from the tree, sling his satchel over his shoulder, and shinny down the trunk. When he reached the bottom, he stood still for another one hundred count, his ears straining for any indication that he was not, in fact, alone. He then stole silently among the bodies of the creatures, slitting each one's throat just to be sure. The last thing he wanted was to be surprised by one of the "corpses" sitting up and smacking him with one of those enormous clubs. The boiled-leather cuirass he wore would provide no protection. The smell of their blood burned his nose, and he wondered what sort of foul sorcery had wrought such creatures.

"Whoa. Did I just think that? What foul sorcery had wrought such creatures?" he mumbled to himself. "I need to get the heck out of here." A crow—was it the same one from the night before?—cawed at him in laughter. "Bah," he grunted at it.

He stopped and took a deep breath to clear his head, then surveyed the surroundings. The fire had burned to embers, so he took a few moments to place new wood on top of the coals and coax a flame back to life. With his dagger, he cut one of the bedrolls—he wasn't sure whose—into strips and wound them around a stout tree branch. He placed that end into the fire and used it as a torch to help him see past the glow of the campfire.

Stu's bow lay in pieces on the ground, the ends still connected by the string. Allison's mace lay trampled in the dirt, and one of the horns from her ridiculous helmet had snapped off. He didn't see it anywhere and hoped that it had gotten lodged in one of the creatures' feet. Their packs and bedrolls were all on the ground, and most important, Jimmy's gigantic two-hander had been left behind as well. Whatever plans the creatures had for his friends didn't involve their possessions. Chuck didn't think those plans included eating them, at least not in the short term. They could have done the eating here if they'd wanted to, and they didn't look the type to care if their food was raw or cooked.

"What to do, what to do?" he said, followed immediately by, "First, stop talking to yourself." He picked up Jimmy's sword to see how heavy it was and was surprised to discover that it didn't feel nearly as hefty as it looked. In fact, as he held it, the blade seemed to shrink into itself until it become a dagger, just the right size for his hand. He gave a low whistle of appreciation, and part of his mind began to figure how much he could sell it for to a fence. He grinned involuntarily. Enough to retire and live a nice long life, surrounded by servants and the finest things money could buy. That much.

He shook his head to clear the thought. "Focus," he said. "Focus. Your friends are in trouble—what are you going to do about it?" The part of him that had begun to surface when they crossed into this fantasy world had already decided: he was willing to say farewell to his friends and go live a life of luxury. That part was, however, overruled with a stern "No!" and sent to sulk in the back of his mind.

The sword's weight had been his biggest concern, and now that that problem had been solved, he collected Allison's mace and helmet, as well as the short sword that Stu had been using to ward off the club blows. Unfortunately, there was nothing worth salvaging from the bow. Any spells placed on it would have been destroyed when the bow itself was broken. It was now nothing more than a bunch of sticks. If Stu was still alive, and he was somehow able to be rescued, he would have to find a new one.

A flash of color caught Chuck's eye, and he went to investigate. Lying in a loose pile were a small number of arrows, which must have fallen out of the quiver attached to Stu's belt as he was manhandled from the campsite. He picked them up and examined them closely, smelling one, placing another against his tongue. "Huh. Yeah, I bet he'll want these," he said, and carefully bundled them in the middle of his bedroll. At the very least they were extraordinarily well made. More likely, they had been imbued with some magic spell that perhaps made them fly farther, or truer, or do more damage, or who knows what.

He gave the campsite one last look to make sure he hadn't missed anything of value. Allison's ring was nowhere to be found, which wasn't particularly surprising. There was no reason for it to have fallen off her finger. TJ's reagent pouch was also absent, and Chuck hoped that it hadn't come loose or been forcibly removed by their attackers. He wasn't sure how many of TJ's spells relied on those focus elements and how many he could cast without them. He shrugged, remembering TJ's lesson from the James Bond books: the pouch wasn't here, so Chuck had to assume that it was still with him. If it wasn't, there was nothing he could do about it.

The last thing he did was rummage through his friends' satchels, commandeering the coin purses and trail rations from each. He would've loved to have eaten some of the rabbit that Stu promised them for the morning, but it was unlikely the snares had survived the nighttime assault. And even if they had, all the smart rabbits were probably miles away. He sat down by the fire and made himself swallow some of the food. He would need the energy, and anyway, he didn't want to follow too closely behind. If they had a rear guard watching for danger, he might get caught, and he didn't think he'd have trouble following their movements, despite his less-than-stellar woodlore. Based on the noise the beasts made as they left, no doubt they were leaving plenty of tracks as they trod through the forest.

After he had eaten his fill, he stood up and checked the bindings of his weapons in their scabbards. "Let's hunt some *orrrrc*, or maybe *kobolllld*," he said in his best Aragorn voice, and let out a giggle. He then dropped his torch into the fire and trotted off into the woods, with nothing but the moon through the branches and the path of trampled foliage to guide him.

CHAPTER 13

The path took Chuck in a southeasterly direction, as opposed to due east, though that only surprised him a little. On the one hand, he was used to a relatively linear story line, and if the story said go east to meet the foozle, by gum, that's what you did. On the other hand, it was all too clear that they weren't following a story line anymore, so he should try to readjust his mental picture of the world. He was still reeling somewhat from the influx of memories—mostly bad ones—from growing up on the streets but was bolstered by the fact that he had survived it all. More than survived—he had thrived. Perhaps more than anyone in the group, he felt like he could take on this new world.

The kobolds didn't get any better at hiding their trail, so he felt comfortable lagging behind. The one or two times that he got close enough to hear their movement ahead he paused to eat and take care of nature's other obligations.

As the day began to brighten—the trees blocked the view of the sun's climb over the horizon—he began to yawn, feeling the fatigue of only a partial night's sleep and a long march. "Man, what I wouldn't do for a Mountain Dew right about now," he said. With a snort, he added, "And some Cheetos." Not long after, his eyes began to lose their ability to focus, and he tripped over a root.

"Ugh. End of the line for now." Hoping that the kidnappers would need to stop and rest at some point, or at least continue to leave a trail, he found another tree in which he could catch a couple hours of sleep. The weight from the extra food and his friends' weapons didn't keep him from making it up the trunk in short order, and after he roped himself in, he shut his eyes and fell asleep.

Almost three hours later, the rogue was greeted by the sound of a crow cawing not too far away. He rubbed his eyes, still itchy from sleep, and then slapped himself in the cheeks lightly several times to bring himself to full alertness. The bird cawed again and flew over to land on the branch upon which he was sitting. It let out another squawk at full volume and then looked him in the eyes, as if to make sure he was really awake.

"You again?" He squinted at the bird. "OK, OK, I hear you," he said grudgingly. "Time to get up, huh? I don't know what it means to you, but yeah, I'm awake."

The bird cocked its head, almost as if to suggest that it wasn't entirely sure it believed him. Chuck stuck his tongue out at it, and it tittered briefly before launching into the air and flying off.

"Well, wasn't that irritating? I could have used another hour or two. But I guess if I'm up, I may as well get moving again."

Once down from his perch, he set off again, following the obvious signs of travel. As he walked he kept his eyes on the ground, looking for some sign that his friends were still alive, or at least still with their captors. It seemed, however, that nothing else had fallen loose after those arrows spilled out of Stu's quiver. On the bright side, he didn't find any chewed-up bones either.

Around midafternoon he heard the sound of rushing water ahead of him. Chuck slowed instinctively, knowing that the noise of the water might mask sounds of a more hostile nature. The trees had begun to thin noticeably, and soon he was able to see the true end of the forest. Creeping forward toward the tree line, he scanned in all directions for signs of danger. When he reached the very edge of the woods, he crouched down behind one of the last trees and looked out.

In front of him, perhaps thirty yards away, was a shallow river. The riverbed was peppered with large rocks that must have been carried downstream during a previous flood; the terrain was otherwise flat, so the boulders couldn't have just fallen from a cliff. On the other side of the river was a rolling plain. There were few trees dotting the landscape, but because of the slight hills, the horizon was relatively close. Similar hills blocked his view upstream, and the river curved around and back into the forest downstream. There was no sign of his quarry.

"Devin's feet," he cursed, and only briefly wondered what it meant and how he had thought to say it.

He darted to the water's edge, hoping for some sort of sign. The bank on the near side showed dozens of footprints spread out over a wide area, so it looked as if the creatures had simply walked across in a herd. He picked his way across the river, and ice-cold droplets splashed up from his steps to land on his hands and cheeks. His boots were well oiled and watertight, so while he could feel the temperature of the water through the leather, his feet remained wonderfully dry. The soles were thick and hard, so he barely felt the gravelly riverbed through them.

When he reached the other shore, his heart sank. While the ground was moist, there were no footprints to be seen. He trotted first downstream and then up a hundred yards or more. Either there was a secret cavern in the riverbed (which he judged unlikely) or they were trudging through the water to hide their movements and make pursuit more difficult. He cursed his laziness and regretted that the bird hadn't woken him up earlier. Casting around hopelessly, he realized he would have to pick one way or the other and hope he was right. He kicked at a rock in frustration and sat down on the bank, placing his face in his palms.

A familiar cawing noise came from above him, and as he lifted his head from his hands, he saw that same bird—or one very similar—circling above him. "OK, so now what, huh?" he shouted. "Even with your help, I *still* overslept!" He reached down to pick up a stone to hurl at the bird and caught a flash of motion in the river. Three quick steps into the water revealed what it was—a buckle attached to a leather strap. It was the light reflecting off the metal that had caught his attention. He recognized it as part of the battle harnesses the kobolds were wearing the day before, and he realized this meant they had gone upstream, not downstream. The leather was damp but not sodden, suggesting it hadn't been in the river for very long. It gave him hope that they were not terribly far away.

He briefly looked back up to see if his bird was still there. It had gone to perch on a rock not far upstream from where he was standing. It cocked its head at him expectantly, then flew off farther upstream. "OK, I get it. Timmy fell down the well again, Lassie, and I've got to go rescue him." He set off at a trot, once again hopeful that he might be able to help his friends after all.

CHAPTER 14

"Oof." The noise returned Allison to consciousness from the daze she had been in for what seemed like eternity. Her head was pounding, and a sharp stone was digging into her left shoulder where it pressed against the ground. From what she could tell, she was inside a large burlap sack, her hands and feet both tied tightly. Small pinpricks of light poked through the fabric, though she couldn't tell if it was only morning or if she had been out longer. A river burbled nearby, and a crow called off in the distance. The only other sounds were the grunting noises of their captors. Allison tried to wiggle herself off the rock and a groan escaped her lips.

Jimmy whispered from nearby. "Allie? Is that you? Are you OK?"

She murmured assent. "Your voice sounds like I feel," she whispered with a chuckle that she immediately regretted. Pain shot up and down her chest, and she only barely kept in a gasp.

"And you sound terrible," she finished once she had caught her breath.

"Tell me about it," Jimmy responded. "At least you went down quickly. I'm pretty sure one of my arms and about a dozen of my ribs are broken. I'm something of a mess over here." Despite his obvious pain, he seemed cheerful enough, which totally blew Allison's mind. As if reading her thoughts, he continued: "The bright side is they haven't killed us yet. So maybe we'll have the chance to enact a daring escape. Or something."

"Quiet, dog," a voice grunted, and Allison heard the unmistakable sound of a boot hitting flesh. Jimmy let out a whoosh of air but otherwise kept silent. With the bag over her body she had no clue if her friend had lost consciousness again or if he was simply following instructions, and she was in no mood to test their captors' patience by asking. She was sure she wouldn't take broken bones nearly as well as the berserker.

Taking a moment to clear her mind, Allison attempted to channel her healing energies toward herself. Clearly, it was somewhat different from curing others. Rather than welling up the energy from inside herself, as she'd done to save TJ's life, she drew the energy into herself from the ground. As the power spread through her limbs, the pain receded, but it was replaced by pins and needles. The magic faded and her body felt almost as good as it had before she'd gone to bed the night before. She had only a few moments to enjoy her new health before a wave of exhaustion passed through her and she drifted into unconsciousness.

CHAPTER 15

As Chuck progressed farther upstream, the terrain became steeper, and therefore more difficult to traverse. Millennia of rushing water had carved its way into the ground, and there was a gradually heightening ridge on either side of the river. Small scrub clung to the sides, though the ground was too rocky to support larger trees. Chuck's bird friend alternated between disappearing into the distance and continuing to hop from rock to rock, leading him farther upriver. He interpreted that to mean that his quarry had not yet left the water, but he still took his time as he went, looking for signs on either bank that boots had exited the river and resumed their trek across dry ground. After a time, when the ridges on either side had gotten steep enough, he stopped looking quite so hard. That many bodies trying to climb out of a gorge would leave some pretty obvious tracks.

Sure enough, when he finally came to the spot where they'd left the river, it was as obvious as he expected. Rough steps had been hewn from the rock walls in what looked like quite a hurry. Stone fragments littered the steps, and a pickaxe bent beyond repair lay cast aside, half-submerged in the rushing water. The air even had the smell of freshly crushed rock to it, a smell that momentarily flooded his mind with memories of treasure-filled caverns. Ever cautious, he took several deep breaths to calm his nerves and focus his hearing before he began climbing the still-damp stairway, one step at a time.

Nearing the top step, he briefly peeked his head over the ridge to get a glimpse of what might be up there waiting for him. At first blush, there was nothing getting ready to bash his head in when he climbed over the top. He took a second, longer look to be sure, and let out a sigh of relief. All that was waiting for him were the remains of a hasty campsite.

The embers of a campfire glowed within a small ring of stones. Larger rocks suitable for sitting were placed in a larger circle around the fire pit. While the ground near the steps was damp, the area close to the flames was completely dry. Chuck surmised that they had taken a few minutes to dry their boots before moving on. If the boots were anything like that harness piece that had come floating down the river, their feet would've been sopping wet after the march upstream.

He was disappointed to discover that there still weren't any signs of his friends, but the fact that the fire still burned indicated he couldn't be very far behind them. The creatures, having hidden their tracks through the water, were apparently no longer concerned about being pursued. The trail was once again absurdly easy to follow. Small stunted trees that looked like cedars sprouted here and there, and low scraggy brush grew between them. A wide path of crunched-down brush led directly away from the camp. Despite the quality of his boots, some water had splashed up over his calves and dripped down into his socks. Chuck took a few moments to warm his own feet by the fire and then set off again.

Determined not to lose his friends again and rely on some bird to find them, he proceeded at a trot. He hoped that any noise he made would be covered up by his quarry's own thudding boots. After about twenty minutes of traveling, he began to hear noises ahead, so he slowed down to keep from running into their rear guard. He still had no idea what they were saying, but they were the same noises he heard earlier at the campsite.

The terrain continued to get rockier as they moved away from the river. In the distance Chuck was able to see mountains rising up into the clouds. "How stereotypical," he mumbled to himself, assuming that was their ultimate destination. "Now all we need are a bunch of saliva-dripping goblins to burst into song and we'll be in Middle Earth."

Night fell, but the creatures kept up their march through the dim light. Darkness had been his friend from childhood, so Chuck allowed himself to get within sight of them. He crept forward until he could see the entire group. Either he had miscounted before or some had split off, because there were fewer than half as many in the group as he expected. Still far too many for him to fight single-handedly—even one would have been impossible—but few enough to make him believe that maybe it wasn't hopeless, particularly if any of his friends were able to help. He was surprised to see no rear guard. Either they were too stupid to have one or they assumed they were home free.

As for his friends, four of the monsters had sacks slung over their shoulders. Assuming that TJ and the rest were in those sacks, that would explain why he hadn't seen any further traces of them after finding Stu's arrows. If TJ and the rest were *not* in those sacks, he was well and truly out of luck. Or rather, *they* were well and truly out of luck. He would just go live a long and fruitful life. The part of his personality he had stuffed into a dark corner perked up hopefully.

One creature near the front barked out a growl, and the group came to a halt. The bags were flung to the ground, and Chuck gave a silent sigh of relief at the muffled groans. His friends were alive! (*Back into the corner with you,* he thought.) The creatures began to mill around—they had decided to camp here for the night. The one who had given the halt order and his companion began chattering back and forth, along with a number of gestures and foot stomping. Quick as a blur, the leader struck out with his club, smacking the other in the side of the head. Taken completely by surprise, the second dropped to the ground and lay still. The leader gave another loud growl, the moaning sacks were once again hoisted over shoulders, and the group continued on.

When the group had left the area, Chuck stole forward to examine the dead creature. There were no identifying marks that he could discern, nor any jewelry to pocket. Whatever the two had disagreed on didn't matter to him. This was just one less thing to worry about while attempting to free his friends. Better safe than sorry, he took the time to slit its throat, then wiped the blade off on its fur and continued on without another look.

The moon was full and high in the sky, bathing everything around him in a soft glow. His eyes, trained through years spent on rooftops and in alleyways, were able to see nearly as well at night as during the daytime. He had also learned through years of experience not to be cocky about what he thought others could or could not do. Chuck assumed that the monsters shared his ability to see in little light, and he acted accordingly.

He maintained his distance so he could hear, and occasionally see, the back end of the group in front of him.

Again the leader barked out a growl and the group stopped. They did not drop the sacks this time, however, which piqued Chuck's interest. He took the risk of getting closer, crouching behind one of the low shrubs dotting the landscape. At once he realized why the creatures hadn't dropped his friends. They weren't stopping to take a breather or to club each other to death. They had reached their destination. A tunnel was carved into a nearby hill, with flaming braziers on either side. Sentries flanked the tunnel as well, and the group's leader strode directly up to one of them. The two exchanged a series of gestures, and then a roared command from the leader set the pack back in motion. They went into the tunnel and out of Chuck's view. Within moments, all that remained were the tunnel entrance, the sentries, and the braziers.

The gears in the little man's mind had begun to spin.

CHAPTER 16

One benefit of being kicked repeatedly is that the boots begin to tear holes in the bag you've been shoved into. At least, that's how Jimmy looked at it as he peered out into the dim torchlight. Resilient as he was, he hadn't lost consciousness from the blows he'd taken after talking to Allison—although, the ache in his head and jaw made him wish he were made of slightly less stern stuff.

The lair they'd been taken to seemed pretty standard by his estimation. There was a large central hall supported by pillars, and in addition to the entrance, there were at least two corridors leading away from it. It was into one of these they were being dragged, and as his head bounced down each step of a too-long descending staircase, he did his best not to whimper. Through one door, down a long corridor, and into a cell . . . it was almost funny how cliché it all was.

The only light in the prison wing was the torch carried by one of his jailers, but it was enough to see that one of the other sacks was tossed roughly through the cell door on the other side of the hall. Rough hands grabbed the sack he was in and yanked it off him. He remained limp, pretending unconsciousness, despite his head cracking once more against the floor. After a brief exchange of grunts, a blade slipped between his wrists and the thong binding his hands fell away. The cell door clanged shut. Footsteps receded and more grunting echoed down the hall before the outer door also closed.

Hoping there wasn't anyone still watching, Jimmy rolled over and gave his wrists a quick massage to get the blood flowing. A torch burned outside the door, shedding meager light into the room through the barred window. With him in the cell lay Allison and Stu—two heaps in opposite corners. Both appeared to be breathing, though Stu looked to be in much worse shape. Maybe, he mused, Allison's less harsh treatment meant chivalry wasn't dead among the kobolds. Still, it wouldn't save them once he got out of this cell. He felt his face turn warm in anger, and it took a few moments of deep breathing to control himself. There was no benefit in letting the bloodrage out now.

He crawled over to Stu first. Blood crusted his face and hands, though the bleeding seemed to have stopped. A quick inspection revealed that most of his upper body was intact but one of his legs was bent at an odd angle. When he probed it gently, Stu's eyes flashed open and a moan escaped his lips.

"Owwwww! Don't do that!" A hand swatted out, slapping Jimmy ineffectually.

"Easy there, Stu," he soothed. "Just giving you a quick rundown. We appear to have arrived at our final destination." He patted his friend on the shoulder.

"Errrg," came the response, and Jimmy was once again reminded of how quickly he healed compared to the rest of the crew. On the one hand, it made it much easier for him to take charge and protect the weaker ones. On the other hand, he sometimes forgot that what would be a minor scratch to him could put someone else out of the fight completely.

"OK, hands off, completely," he apologized.

"Why are we even alive? Not that I'm entirely sure I want to be." A pause. "Where are the others?"

"As for the first, I don't know. But we are, and so we're going to get out of here. As for the second, Allison is snoozing over there. She looks to be in much better shape than you are—I think she healed herself a bit on the trip, but it took a lot out of her. We should let her sleep as much as possible to get her energy back. Someone else is across the hall—my guess is TJ. I was the last one standing, and I never saw Chuckles enter the fight. Hopefully he got away."

"Hopefully he got eaten, is more like it," Stu countered. "I didn't get along super well with my brothers and sisters—too different, you know—but at least they always had my back."

"I don't think he woulda made much difference in that fight. I don't know if *anything* coulda made much difference in that fight."

Stu was unimpressed. "Yeah, well, he should have gone down with the rest of us."

"Think of it this way. Maybe he's out there right now, trying to find a way to come save us. He's got quite a few tricks up his sleeve. I bet he'll come through."

"Hmpf." With a grunt, Stu rolled over, ending the conversation.

"I sure hope you're out there, little man," Jimmy murmured to himself. "I'm not going to be able to save the day this time."

CHAPTER 17

Just outside the tunnel, Chuck smiled. While others might have been daunted by the prospect of a lair that no doubt concealed many more of the kobolds than were in the raiding party, he wasn't bothered. While others might have seen this as a trap waiting to spring on them, Chuck knew better. This was a puzzle, and puzzles have solutions. He had made a career of solving just these sorts of puzzles, first in the city where he was trained, and then in the wilds as a member of an adventuring company.

His first order of business was getting into the tunnel unseen. If the moon weren't so bright he could have just sneaked around them, trusting his instincts to keep his footfalls silent. Even with the moon as bright as it was, he figured he had a fifty-fifty chance. Fifty-fifty was good enough when he knew he had backup available to bail him out of trouble if he failed. But it wasn't near enough when he *was* the backup, and if he got caught they were all doomed. *Doomed*. The word triggered a memory in his head, but he couldn't put his finger on it. He shrugged.

The hill that the tunnel was carved into had a steep face. Steep, but not sheer, and this made a huge difference. He had rappelled from rooftops into windows many times in the past without incident. The slight grade made his lack of a rope less of an issue than if the wall were sheer. He slowly circled around to the side and examined the ground between him and the entrance. He would be completely exposed while he crossed the space, and a loss of footing could be deadly. There were patches of gravel here and there, but it was mostly solid rock, worn by the movement of ancient rivers, with slight grooves where the rock had been weaker and more easily etched. He smiled at the extra traction it would provide.

Before he left the cover of the shrubs, he let his eyes drift over the area between him and the tunnel. He had always found it interesting that dark vision was better at the periphery of his sight than directly in the middle—his science teacher, Mrs. Morris, had said it had something to do with rods and cones or something. Anyway, he couldn't count the number of times he had spotted something just off center that he had missed when staring straight at it. His extra diligence paid off, because he spotted the outline of a third sentry at the top of the hill, looking out for anyone who planned to do exactly what he planned on doing. He smiled again.

Very carefully, Chuck reached into his satchel and removed a hard wooden case about the size of his hand. Inside were several small black darts with black fletching. He chose one and inspected it closely, then gently closed the case, making sure the latch was secure. He reached into his satchel again and peeled back a hidden flap, exposing a small stiff pocket. From it, he removed a small vial, smaller than his pinky finger. His eyes lit up and a grin stretched across his face. Out of habit he looked over his shoulder to make sure no one was watching. Even among the other thieves in the guild, this sort of thing was frowned upon, since it tended to bring unnecessary attention. His friends had no idea he'd worked as a guild assassin, and he had no intention of telling them. He still felt guilty about what he had done in the guild's employ—that was the true reason he'd fled Westmarch.

Chuck gave the vial a slight shake and then unstopped it. He raised it to his nose and briefly sniffed. The scent made him swoon for a moment. "Yeah," he said to himself. "That's what I'm talking about." And while he carried lingering guilt about some of the contracts he'd taken as an assassin, he wasn't going to let that stop him now from using the skills he'd spent years perfecting. He dipped the dart into the vial and swirled it around briefly before pulling it out and blowing on it to dry the venom. Very carefully, he restoppered the vial, returned it to the hidden pocket, and then removed one more item, a short tube. With a flick of the wrist, the tube telescoped as four sections slid out from the inside. In total, it was perhaps two feet long. He placed the dart in one end, careful to keep the poisoned point from touching the tube as it slid in. He'd once made the mistake of accidentally licking venom from the end of the blowgun. It was nearly his last mistake.

The weapon primed, he slung the satchel back over his shoulder and scanned the area for other places of concealment. Whoever had designed the defenses was careful to create wide fields of vision for the sentries—virtually all the scrub brush had been hacked away between him and the tunnel's entrance. A low bush sprouted roughly half the distance between him and the sentry, but the space between it and him was too exposed. If the night were cloudy, or there were no moon, he knew he would have no trouble crossing the distance. As things stood, however, he was going to have to take the longer shot. Luckily, there was no wind that could send the dart off target.

He got down on his belly and gauged the distance to the sentry. He lifted himself up on his elbows and placed the blowgun in the crook of a branch to stabilize it. Looking down the barrel, he noted his view was blocked by a few leaves that poked out of the bush's branches, so he reached out to pluck them. The distance was longer than he would have preferred, so before putting his mouth to the rod he took several deep breaths to spread out his lungs. Saying a silent prayer to Mairead, goddess of tricks, he took one last breath and blew through the weapon, sending the black barb of death streaking toward his target.

He knew that he had hit his mark when the kobold flailed an arm and reached toward its neck. The poison he had chosen was a fast-acting one that paralyzed the respiratory system, then the rest of the muscles. Hardly a pleasurable way to die, he reflected, and not a method he had used often. When he would take contract jobs, he tried to use poisons that were slow-acting and painless—not to mention exponentially less expensive—ideally killing overnight while the subject was sleeping. That had been years ago, though. Now if he had to resort to poisons, he typically didn't have a few hours to wait for someone to keel over, nor could he afford to let the target get the alarm out. By the time the sentry realized he had been attacked, his lungs had shut down, making it impossible to call out. By the time he realized he couldn't call out, his limbs had stopped working, keeping him from even throwing a rock or waving a torch. In moments, the figure toppled backward and out of Chuck's sight.

He heaved a sigh of relief. If the sentry had fallen in the other direction, he would have landed right at the feet of his comrades, ruining any possibility of rescue. The part of Chuck that had been toying with the idea of a long and healthy life was disappointed, but the part of him trying to rescue his friends told the former to shut up. Before he got up to move, he took the time to wipe off his blowgun and collapse it back into its shorter form, then put it back into his bag. Chuck sat and waited, counting to one hundred once again. It was possible there were other sentries up there out of view, and if there were, he didn't want them to discover the body while he was exposed on the hillside.

When he finished counting, he carefully stepped out into the open, eyes searching for potential danger, as well as a path to safety should that danger materialize. When he heard no shouts of alarm, he began to scuttle toward the top of the tunnel. The closer he got to the entrance, the steeper the incline became, so he had to turn and face the wall and move sideways. The last ten yards were very steep, so he had to press his body against the wall and slide his feet. This was the part he was most anxious about—all it would take was for either of the sentries to look up. He was a sitting duck.

At last he reached the mouth of the tunnel, where he turned, his back against the face once again. The smoke from the braziers below burned his nose, and he fought the urge to sneeze by biting on the tip of his tongue. Looking down into where the tunnel opened from the hillside, he saw nothing but darkness inside, as the light from the braziers did not extend very far. Assuming its floor was level, the drop was perhaps twelve or fifteen feet—something he had done many times before. His knees would need to be replaced when he got old, or perhaps healed if he never made it back to the real world, but for now they were good at absorbing the shock. He dangled his feet over the edge, drew the magical dagger that Jimmy's sword had become, and took a deep breath. Scooching slightly forward, he dropped silently down into the tunnel's mouth.

He began moving as soon as he landed, darting sideways to press his back against the tunnel wall and blend deeper into the shadows. There were no sounds, and no sign of movement, either from deeper within or from the guards standing watch outside. Hugging the wall, he crept into the hill. The flicker of light ahead revealed a sharp bend and what was most likely a torch just beyond it. Cautiously, he peeked around the corner.

The tunnel looked to have been naturally occurring, at least near the entrance. Chuck noticed, however, that the walls and floor became smoother as he progressed. By the time he had made it to the bend, they became like masonry walls, flat to the touch, and the corner was perfectly cut. One thing was for sure—this wasn't made by some random tribe of humanoids living in caves and raiding for food and riches. Rather, it had been constructed by skilled hands, and designed to last for the long term. Whether or not the kobolds who captured his friends were the builders or just squatters remained to be seen.

He peeked around the corner and was surprised to discover that the quality of the masonry abruptly stopped ten feet or so away. Beyond that point, the walls of the tunnel looked as if they had been hammered repeatedly with sledges—or perhaps, he thought wryly, been blasted with haphazard use of TNT. Twenty feet farther, a small chamber had been roughly excavated, with an ironbound door set in the far wall. Judging from the chunks of rubble littering the floor, Chuck figured the work had been done recently. The monsters that had abducted his friends must have found the beginnings of a back door to an underground fortress and forced their way in. Not particularly elegant, but effective.

Chuck slipped around the corner and edged down the tunnel and into the room, looking for possible foes or peepholes through which a sentry could be looking. He discovered none, which didn't really surprise him. The three outside the tunnel would theoretically provide ample warning, and any other guards outside that door would merely get butchered if enemies came down the tunnel. Approaching the door, he first put his ear against the keyhole on the off chance he could hear any noises on the other side. The thudding of his heart was the only sound he heard, and he forced himself to take several deep breaths to calm his nerves. Confident that he wasn't going to be surprised by someone opening the door, he examined it closely.

The wood was oak, and the size of the bindings and the rivets within them indicated that the door was thick—at least half a foot, perhaps more. He had no expectation of being able to break it down, but it was one more piece of information he could use. They keyhole itself was large, suggesting a heavy internal bolting mechanism. He nodded at that. Larger bolts required larger keys, but that also provided more wiggle room for lockpicking. Tentatively, he slid a narrow tool down the crack between the door and the frame. It met resistance exactly where the bolt should be, signifying it was indeed locked. If they had turned the bolt, the door was almost certainly barred from the other side, so even if he managed to pick the lock, he still wouldn't be able to get through. Stonemasons the kobolds were not, but they installed solid doors. This was literally a dead end.

"OK, think," he murmured to himself, knowing that the sound wouldn't pass through six-plus inches of wood. He didn't have a tool long and sturdy enough to raise a bar on the other side of the door. So that seemed like a bust. He looked around, but the chamber was otherwise empty, and the ceiling was not especially high. He couldn't just hide behind something and wait to slip in the next time the door opened up. There wasn't a lot to work with.

He turned his attention to the smoother walls of the passage, hoping to find the telltale crack that indicated a hidden door. It was clear that the kobolds had found a dead end at the point in the tunnel where the walls transitioned from smooth to rough, then hammered away, extending the tunnel, until they busted through into the main chamber. They slapped on a door, and *voilà!*—instant entryway.

But it didn't make sense that there would be a finely crafted passage in the hill that led only to a dead end in the first place. All the recent digging meant that the bad guys hadn't found a secret door, and after ten minutes of searching, Chuck finally concluded he wasn't going to either.

He leaned against the wall and slid down to a sitting position. "Now what am I gonna do?"

He didn't relish the thought of sneaking back past those sentries. He could poison one but was no match for a toe-to-toe fight against the other. His only option was to go forward. The trick was finding a way to do so before someone decided to walk down the passageway.

He stared at the opposite wall for a time, letting his mind wander. Dots began to appear in his field of vision, so he closed his eyes and shook his head to clear them. When he opened them again, he discovered that the dots were still there. Faint, but definitely there. Scrambling up, he fixed his eye on one of the dots and stepped over to it, putting his finger right where he had seen it. Up close, it didn't seem to still be there, but he knew better than to ignore it. He pulled his dagger back out and poked with it. A little mortar chipped off, which surprised him. His blade shouldn't have been strong enough to cut rock by a long shot. He cut at it some more, and soon a perfectly round hole the size of a quarter was revealed. Thinking that it must be hiding a trigger for a secret door, he began exploring it with his finger. A niggling voice in the back of his head said it could be a trap, but he dismissed it. He was plum out of choices at this point.

With a little more prodding, his finger pushed through and into an open space. He cleaned out the hole as best he could, first with his finger and then by blowing lightly into it. No matter how much he played with the inside of the hole, he was unable to discover any hidden triggers or catches. He stepped down the hallway a bit to give himself some perspective and tried to identify where the other dots might have been. Now that he knew more or less what to look for, the others became clear. They were regularly spaced and in a perfect vertical line from a foot off the floor up to a foot short of the ceiling. Marking the next higher one with his eye, he returned and carved out the next hole, finding it to be exactly like the first. There were a couple inches of mortar, then emptiness behind it.

"Very interesting," he said to himself, and stepped back again to survey the situation. A series of equally spaced holes bored into a wall in a straight line from floor to ceiling. He grinned. "Oh, no they didn't." He approached the holes again and looked straight up at the ceiling. "Oh, yes they did!" He stopped short and looked around, worried that in his enthusiasm he might have given himself away. While having guards come charging out the door would take care of the locked-door problem, it would create new problems that would be significantly worse.

Taking out Jimmy's dagger-sword, he jammed it into the higher of the two holes, all the way to the hilt. He hadn't expected it would go all the way in, but the magic must have adapted to fit it the same way it had when he first picked it up and it became a dagger. The hole into which he had shoved the blade was about chest height.

He nodded. "Yeah, that'll do." He squatted for a moment and then leapt straight up, landing on the hilt and balancing easily on one foot. TJ may have gained some knowledge, and Jimmy some strength, but Chuck had the agility of a cat. Or at least a cat burglar.

It took only a few seconds of poking at the ceiling to find where the trapdoor was concealed directly above his head. A little scraping revealed a keyhole, and within seconds he had the lock picked and the trapdoor pushed up and open. There was darkness behind the hole, so Chuck dropped back down to the ground to fetch a torch from one of the sconces, then tossed it up and into the opening. He hoped that what he had found was an escape route and not a sally port, from which to pour boiling oil on invaders—or he might find something horribly flammable up there. Glancing around, he discovered that he'd created quite a mess on the floor with all the scraping he had done on the ceiling. He stepped over to where the mortar chips lay and kicked them into the recently excavated portion of the corridor. With all the rubble already on the floor, the chips would be invisible even to someone looking for them. There was nothing to be done about the holes he had dug in the wall, so he just hoped no one would notice.

He pulled the magic dagger out of the hole and sheathed it, then backed down the passage a bit. He darted forward and leapt at the wall, using it as a springboard and launching himself up into the hole in the ceiling. His fingers grabbed just the edge of the opening, and he pulled himself up with minimal scrambling. He was pleased to discover the torch was still burning, and it revealed a small room with a hallway leading away from it. He lowered the trapdoor silently, took the torch, and set off to find his friends.

CHAPTER 18

The tunnel had a low ceiling, reinforcing Chuck's original belief that dwarves had built the complex. He idly wondered what happened to the original owners and if they had left any of their treasures hidden away in other secret chambers—he made a mental note to keep his eyes peeled. He was going to have to search pretty hard to find his friends anyway, so there wouldn't be any harm in exploring completely, would there?

It looked as if the tunnel hadn't been used in a very long time. Chuck's boots left footprints in the thick dust that had settled over the years. He found it interesting that the quality of the stonework in this emergency tunnel was every bit as polished as in the main entrance passageway below. It made him remember how his real-life dad complained about not being able to find good workers nowadays. Here were people who took pride in their work. The thought of his dad made him stumble. They weren't exactly close, but the idea of never seeing him again gave him pause. "One more reason to rescue the crew and get us out of here, I guess," he muttered.

He continued on his path for twenty minutes without seeing any signs of an exit. He hadn't really expected there to be more than one; this sort of thing was typically reserved for a royal family to escape while their loyal subjects fought to the death. He smiled, realizing just how cynical he had become. Those years living on the street in Westmarch must have done it to him. Was that before or after his father complained about good workers? He shook his head and continued on.

He finally came to a dead end. The back of the wall was rough stone, which momentarily made him fear that the tunnel had been left unfinished and no second door was ever put in. After a few moments of heavy breathing, he reconsidered. If this really was the escape shaft for someone important, they wouldn't want the door into their chambers to be obvious, just in case someone else was as clever as Chuck and found the trapdoor in the ceiling. It occurred to him that if he were designing it, the tunnel would purposely overshoot the escape hatch, and the unfinished dead end would add to the illusion that there was, in fact, no portal.

He shuffled back down the tunnel, dragging his boots to try to reveal any seams in the rock hidden by the layers of dust. His fingertips traced along the wall to feel any inconsistency in the stonework. He cursed when he found the start to his own footprint trail in the dust, then turned back to retrace his steps, this time with his hand touching the opposite side. Once again he made it the entire distance without finding anything that would suggest a hidden door.

Tears of frustration stung his eyes. He had spent an hour already trying to find the exit with no success while his friends were trapped somewhere below, having who knows what done to them. He had been so sure of himself, so cocky when he found the escape hatch. How could he be stymied now? Was it possible that they never actually *had* finished the tunnel? That there was no door for him to find? He took a deep breath and smelled something new: burning wood.

Puzzled, he examined his torch, but the wooden handle had been wrapped in oil-soaked rags. The rags were burning, not the wood itself. Looking around for the source of the smell, he noticed that the portion of the ceiling directly above where he had stopped had begun to smolder. As a test, he took several steps back down the passageway and held his torch to the ceiling there as well. While the stone blackened, it didn't burn in the same manner. Chuck brought the magic dagger back out and started chipping away at the area where the ceiling had begun to char. It wasn't long before he had the outline of yet another trapdoor exposed, and after a little more scraping, the entire door was visible. He saw no lock to pick; the trapdoor must open from within. Having no other option, he brought the torch back up, and as the wood charred he dug at it with the dagger. Soon he had a hole big enough for his arm to reach through to unbolt the door.

Up through the trapdoor he went, finding himself in a small room with a single door leading from it. On each of the walls hung clothes from rods and hooks, and along the floor were court shoes in dozens of shapes, though both the clothes and shoes had long gone out of style. The room had a musty smell to it, suggesting that it had been a long time indeed since anyone had put it to use besides long-term storage. A casual inspection of the clothing revealed that it was made of the finest materials—silks and furs. Chuck rifled through several before he stopped, his eyes lighting up. He pulled out a brocaded tunic of rich reds and purples that screamed wealth. More important than the colors, the buttons down the front glinted in the torchlight. He put one between his teeth and bit down slightly, then grinned. "Yeah. Gotta search everywhere, don't I?" He cleared a space on the floor and gently laid down the torch, then deftly cut all the gold buttons off the garment and tucked them away in a pouch.

Despite the fact that the closet had clearly long since been abandoned, he was careful as he cracked open the door. As expected, the room was vacant and there was a layer of dust on the floor. Also as expected, the room's opulence was such that it could only have been the living chamber of royalty. Gold was everywhere, and the wood carvings were exquisite. His eyes widened. He suddenly felt very foolish for taking the time to swipe the buttons. He opened the first drawer he found and discovered a small felt bag within. Inside the bag was a king's ransom in cut gemstones. *"Niiiice,"* he said, tucking it away as well.

"OK," he mumbled, "so now that I've enriched myself through public service, let's see if I can't find some friends to rescue." He opened the only other door in the room and peeked out, finding yet another hallway. This one went in both directions, and after a quick "Eeny meeny . . . ," he headed left. In his experience, these sorts of compounds tended to be designed in one of two ways. In some, the royal suite was situated smack-dab in the middle, with everything else radiating out from it. In others, it was in the very top or very bottom, as far as possible from the entrance to make protecting the royals easier in case of attack. Chuck guessed that this one followed the latter pattern, since after entering the cavern he had twice climbed up to get to where he was, and the entrance he had used was relatively high on the hill face. All he had to do was find some stairs heading down, and whether left or right, he would come across them sooner or later.

So if he assumed that he was on the upper levels, it made things easy—the only stairs he would find would take him in the direction in which his friends were being held. The trick would be figuring out just how far down they'd be locked up, but that was a bridge he'd have to cross when he came to it. The creatures obviously weren't using all the available space—these rooms proved that to be true—so he hoped it wouldn't take him long to find the rest of the group. It was surprising that no one had looted the royal chambers. Chuck patted the gems tucked away and mentally added, *Before now.*

With years of experience exploring underground tunnels such as these, Chuck was able to determine the hall had a slight downward slant. Doors sprouted off to the sides, but after exploring four or five of them, he stopped bothering to check. They all seemed to be either storerooms with commodities long since spoiled, or the modest living chambers of those who were there to serve the royal family. He came to a set of stairs leading down, which he took, and discovered another hallway with rooms much like the ones upstairs. There was also a kitchen and what looked to be a small barracks. This last room he took the time to search for anything that could help him free his friends, but the soldiers stationed there had long since taken all of their gear with them.

At the end of this second hallway, approximately beneath where the royal chamber was, he came to a wall with a stone door. A sturdy oak bar lay across it, preventing entry from the other side. Chuck examined the area directly surrounding the door and discovered a peephole off to one side. Through the hole he could see an enormous gallery with dozens of pillars; the room was illuminated by hundreds of torches. It appeared he had found the bad guys. The kobolds moved back and forth through the chamber. Twice one of them walked right in front of his peephole without giving the door a single glance. Chuck deduced that either they had tried to break down the door and failed or didn't even know it existed.

He went back to look at the door, particularly where its hinges were attached and where the bindings for the oaken bar were bolted to the wall. They were completely flush and showed no sign of wear or buckling, which meant that the kobolds hadn't even bothered trying to knock it in. With the numbers that he had seen through the peephole and at the attack, he found it hard to believe that they couldn't have bashed it in if they'd put their mind to it. It must be hidden by something.

There was no way he was going to try to open the door while the beasts were walking around just outside, so he would have to wait until the activity decreased. Kobolds were nocturnal creatures, so he must have gotten here right around lunchtime. He figured it would be a good eight hours before things would settle down enough for him to explore. It was fortuitous that he and his friends would be the most alert when their foes were the most tired. They would have the upper hand if it came to a fight.

To pass the time, he began rummaging around the adjacent chambers in the hope of finding something interesting. The people who lived back here seemed to have left in something of a hurry. All of the living chambers still had clothes in them, just as with the royal bedroom upstairs. The barracks was empty, but that made sense because the soldiers likely had living chambers in other parts of the complex and only brought their required kit when on assignment protecting the royals. That didn't explain why the trapdoor in the escape hatch was also barred from the inside, but he put it aside as something to pursue if he managed to survive the rescue attempt.

He retraced his steps upstairs and began a more thorough search of the royal bedchamber. There were candles placed strategically around the room, and he lit them to keep from having to hold the torch while he searched. In moments, the entire room was awash in a warm glow. The clothes were short and the boots were long, another sign that the former occupants were dwarves. Much of the clothing had been eaten through by bugs, leaving it worthless. There were several more sets of clothing that exhibited golden buttons, but after he found the bag of gems, the buttons just seemed like overkill. A small bookshelf in the corner boasted an assortment of heavy bound books with titles in several languages. He ran his finger along their spines, but none of them seemed particularly interesting. The history of so-and-so. A book on astronomy. A book of genealogies. Perhaps they were valuable to a bookseller, but they were too bulky and were just as likely to be worthless, so he left them where they lay. He had hoped that he'd find something that TJ would deem worthwhile, but unfortunately, none of the books were titled *Really Cool Magic Spells Your Friend Doesn't Already Know*, so he was out of luck.

A large tapestry displaying a dragon breathing fire from the top of a mountain hung on the wall opposite the bookshelf. A sly smile crept over Chuck's face. He padded over to it and gingerly lifted it away from the wall. He shook his head in disbelief at just how stereotypical it was to place a hidden vault behind a tapestry in the king's room. It was one of those things that people laughed about when he was training: *Don't forget to look behind the tapestry!* He was about to pull the fabric aside when a gut feeling stopped him. He slowly released his hold on the cloth and turned back toward the bookcase. Crouching, he walked around the bed and over to the space directly opposite the vault door.

There, just above the bookcase (which would be about chest high for a dwarf), was a series of small holes running horizontally along the wall. He removed a long, skinny tool from his satchel and carefully slid it into one of the holes. About three inches in, it met resistance for a moment and then slid slightly to the side before going in another couple inches and then stopping: darts. Chuck nodded and withdrew the tool. Giving it a slight sniff, he recoiled at the sensation of fire shooting up his nostrils and fell back on his haunches. He shook his head, recognizing that smell. It appeared that the king wanted his robbers to die slowly, in pain. Not a professional's poison.

He pulled the books off a shelf and stacked them on top of the bookcase so that they covered the holes and then nodded at his handiwork. The discovery of the darts meant that the entire area warranted a much more thorough search before trying to open the vault. They may not have stopped at a single trap, and the next one could kill him just as dead. A search for more holes yielded nothing, so he proceeded to check the ceiling directly above the tapestry. His search of the ceiling was just to be safe; after the poison-dart trap, it was unlikely the ceiling would also be rigged, since replacing ceiling stones was a lot harder than rearming a spring trigger. But he searched it anyway. One thing he'd learned about royals over his long career was that when it was someone else's job to do something—like resetting a ceiling stone—the difficulty of the effort wasn't a consideration.

As expected, that search yielded nothing. He decided it was time to approach the vault. He grasped the tapestry firmly by a bottom corner and, standing to the side, yanked it as hard as he could. The fabric popped out of its bindings in the wall, and a burst of flame shot out from the wall behind it, straight at the spot where someone would've been standing had they pulled down the tapestry from the middle. He nodded and went to smother a small fire that had broken out on a rug. When the black streaks in his vision caused by the flare had disappeared, he slowly examined the vault door. There were three keyholes visible, and a small depression that acted as a door handle. Again Chuck put his nose to the test, and after smelling the door, it gave him the all clear. He then fetched a candelabra to give himself more light and discovered slight discoloration in the area of the handle. He held his breath and placed a candle flame directly on the indentation. A black smoke curled up, and he immediately threw his other arm over his nose and mouth and backed away. The smoke curled upward and was whisked away by some invisible ventilation system. He liberated the pillowcase from one of the pillows on the bed and set it aside to wrap his hand in later when he was ready to open the door.

Having decided all the traps had been dealt with, he approached the locks. It was possible that all three locks were legit, but it seemed more likely to him that at least one was a decoy, and if someone tried to open the wrong one, either another trap would spring or some other fail-safe device that made the vault impossible to open would trigger. His first inclination was to use the trick he had before, where he slid something in the crack to find the lock. But the seam between the door and the wall was too tight. The next thing he tried was blowing softly into each of the three locks and listening to the sound it made. Different tumblers whistled different ways when you blew through them, and that made it easier to select the correct tool for the job. Unfortunately, there was nothing that suggested one lock was real and the others weren't. Chuck took out one of his tools reluctantly and gently probed the upper lock. He hoped he would be able to tell the real lock from the fake without triggering whatever unpleasantness was in store for would-be thieves. Frowning, he moved to the second lock, and then to the third. All three felt identical.

So either all three of the locks were real, none of the locks were real, or whoever had designed this was extremely clever. Unwilling to back down from a challenge, he got to work. The upper lock provided virtually no challenge whatsoever. It reminded him of the training locks that he'd learned on years ago. Not meant to be difficult, they let the guild masters know who had ability and who definitely did not. The tumblers moved into place, the bolt clicked aside, and a series of thumps from behind him indicated that the poisoned arrows had been launched—and blocked by the books he had stacked in front of the holes.

"Oh, so that's how we're going to play, huh?" This troubled him. If there were three locks, it suggested that there were three traps as well, not including the fire trap that was tied to the tapestry. His internal clock told him he still had plenty of time before the kobolds started going to bed, so he performed another examination of the area. It was then that he noticed the small hole at the base of the wall, directly beneath the vault entrance. *"Aha!"* he exclaimed. He commandeered another pillowcase and stuffed it down into the hole. "There's number two." He frowned. "But where's number three?"

After twenty minutes, Chuck was unable to find signs of another trap. Shaking his head, he concluded that there really were only two. He reasoned that when you included the flame trap and the contact poison, there were four traps in total, which was pretty respectable, even for a royal vault. He began working on the second lock, and when it finally clicked, he heard a whooshing noise, and the pillowcase he had stuck into the hole in the floor began to smoke. With Jimmy's magical dagger, which he figured was impervious to just about anything, he pulled the fabric back out and held it up. A green sludgy liquid oozed from it, sputtering and spurting as it went. He tossed the cloth aside and watched the ooze dissolve it completely, then settle in a pool on the floor. Acid traps were rarely deadly, but they could really ruin your day, especially if you didn't get your clothes off in time.

With a silent prayer, he began to work on the third lock. It too was well beneath his skill, and it soon gave a resounding click with just a little bit of wiggling. He tensed, waiting for something to happen that would kill or maim or at least embarrass him, but nothing did. "Huh. Well, that was anticlimactic," he said. A loud grating noise from above sent him scurrying backward to hide behind the bed. Several seconds later, the ceiling tile directly above the vault door fell to the ground, where it shattered with a loud crash. He hoped that the sound didn't carry all the way down to the kobolds, and he sent a prayer of thanks to Mairead for the failure of the trap to spring as designed. Chuck had dismissed the prospect of a falling ceiling trap; he would have been squashed flat if it had fallen quickly and silently.

So he had gotten the three locks open, and managed to evade the traps, by guile and by luck. All that was left was to open up the door and see what was inside. Remembering the contact poison, he used the first pillowcase to pull open the door. It glided open on silent hinges, revealing a small room within. He cautiously took the cloth in his hand, which was now permanently tainted, and laid it on the stone floor away from the carpet. He then took a candle and set it on fire, burning away any poison that had rubbed onto it. That sort of attention to detail was what separated short- and long-careered rogues.

He entered the vault and let out a barking laugh. While the room wasn't empty, it certainly wasn't bursting with riches. Several small bags of coins were stacked in one corner, and a gorgeously wrought suit of plate armor stood on a rack in the other. The armor was built for someone of dwarven build, so there was no thought of Chuck donning it, even if he knew how to fight in such bulky gear. One thing did catch his attention almost immediately. A curved bow, built for dwarven hands, rested against the back wall. What was most interesting was that the bow was already strung, and even Chuck knew that wasn't a good thing to do to a bow: it would eventually lose its strength if permanently bent. He tentatively picked it up and drew the string back experimentally. It felt much easier than he would have expected, confirming his suspicion that it had been ruined. On a lark, he picked up an arrow stacked nearby and nocked it to the bow. He drew the string back and released it, sending the arrow flying out of the vault and across the bedroom. To his amazement, the arrow actually lodged itself in the stone wall. It occurred to him that the bow hadn't been ruined after all—it was magic! "Not the size he's used to, but I bet Stu could have some fun with this." He took the bow out and leaned it against the door that led into the hall.

Much as he had been hoping for a magic ring or a bottle with a djinn in it, he had to be satisfied with just the bow. The gems in his pouch were all the wealth he could ask for, and he had already dismissed the armor. Chuck turned back out of the vault and went to lie down on the bed. He had quite a few hours left before he needed to get moving, so he decided to catch a little shut-eye. He lay down on the bed but didn't get under the covers. Not knowing what had happened to these people, he didn't want to be presumptuous, or to bring any bad luck upon himself. Stealing treasures was one thing. Stealing someone's *home* was different. Even if he was just borrowing it, the spirits of the dead were often irrational.

He let his mind wander for a while, thinking back through what he had seen since entering the dwarven compound. He had the sense that he was missing something, but he often had that sense, even when he wasn't. That said, he was sure he wasn't missing anything before the ceiling block almost brained him. Those sorts of senses were hardly reliable.

He sat bolt upright and ran back over to the vault. He looked at the bags of coins and shook his head. "No, it's not that." He looked back at the suit of armor and how it was mounted to the rack. It seemed permanently attached to the ground, which was an odd thing for the builders to have done, since there wouldn't always be armor in the vault and it was a waste of otherwise valuable space. The rogue examined the base closely, then stood up and took a step back, considering the armor as a whole. When he reached out and lifted the left arm, a loud click echoed through the little room. He looked back over his shoulder to discover that a small hole had opened in the wall. Inside was a glittering amulet on a chain that looked exactly the right size for someone named Chuck. Grinning, he took it, then went back to the bed. He was asleep within moments.

CHAPTER 19

"Allison! Allison . . . wake up!" The words drifted out of the darkness, accompanied by a light slapping on one of her cheeks.

"Five more minutes, Dad," she grumbled, halfheartedly pawing at the air in the direction of the voice. It was only after a good deal of shoulder shaking that she reluctantly opened her eyes. It was still oppressively dark, and she wasn't lying in her bed but on a thin pile of straw covering a solid, uncomfortable floor. The events of the prior day flashed back through her mind: passing in and out of unconsciousness as she bounced back and forth against some creature's back. Some really smelly creature's back. She jerked straight up, her head momentarily clear. Jimmy sat next to her, his hand still on her shoulder.

Her eyes darted about the gloom, fixing on each of her friends in turn. It took only a moment to do the head count before she blurted, "Where's Chuck?" More urgently, she asked, *"And where's TJ? We have to find him!"* She began to get up, but dizziness swept through her. That, combined with the large berserker's restraining hand, plopped her back onto her rear.

"Shh," Jimmy whispered, not unkindly. "Sit still. You're recovering from your healing, so chill for a few minutes. If you pass back out it won't do us any good at all." He kept his hand on her throughout a couple ineffectual struggles until she gave up the battle and heaved out a sigh.

"OK," she finally said, yanking her arm away from him. "I'm chill. Now answer my question. Where are they?"

"I was awake when we were brought down, so I know that TJ is across the hall. They must have wanted to make sure we couldn't untie or ungag or unwhatever him, so there are two doors between us and him." He paused a heartbeat, then continued softly, "Chuck ditched us. Again."

"What do you mean ditched us?" Allison shot back angrily. "He wouldn't do that!" Jimmy just looked at her until she added uncertainly, "Would he?"

From the other side of the cell, Stu spoke up. "Of course he would. He did it back at the brigand camp, and we all know he's never wanted a stand-up fight. He was up in that tree of his, watching the whole time, and never said a word. At least not before I got knocked out." This was the most Stu had said at once since the brigand camp, and Allison could hear the venom dripping from his words.

Jimmy put his hand back on her shoulder. "Whatever happened, he's not here. We have more important things to worry about right now. My body's already begun to heal itself some, but Stu's pretty beaten up, and we haven't heard a thing from TJ, so he's going to need some help too. Then we've got to find a way out of here. I don't know why they kept us alive, but there's no way I'm going down without a fight."

Allison took a deep breath and nodded, then tried once again to stand. This time, her friend's large hands helped her rise, steadying her as dizziness came and went. Three strides across the cell brought her to where Stu lay in a heap. She crouched next to him.

"Tell me where it hurts," she said, followed by, "the worst."

Stu looked back at her with a wry grin. "One leg feels like it's broken. And maybe a few ribs. Arms are OK. Head is . . . well, it's pretty rough."

"OK, sit tight," she said, placing her hands on his injured leg and channeling her healing gifts. His leg grew warm to the touch, then hot, but she held on until she knew that the bones had knitted. Sparing a quick glance toward his face, she saw his jaw clenched and pain lines etched into his forehead. When it was all done, they both let out sighs of relief. "How's that?" Allison asked.

"Much better. I'm sure I can walk on it now, maybe even run. But," he added with a grimace, "if it's all the same to you, let's leave the ribs for another time. That was pretty intense."

Allison shook her head. "Even if you wanted it, I couldn't give it. I'm just about toast myself. I need another nap. If you guys figure out a way to get us out of here, let me know." She let out a big yawn and was soon curled up on top of the straw.

"You got it," Jimmy muttered, and returned to the cell door to inspect it for weaknesses yet again. He hadn't found anything, but at least it passed the time.

CHAPTER 20

Chuck sat up in bed, alert. He didn't know for sure how much time had passed but trusted himself to have woken to the internal alarm clock he'd set before going to sleep. He found it funny how just a few days before he could barely get himself out of bed to make it to school. Now that the stakes had been raised, his body had adapted. He swung his feet over the side of the bed and sprang up. Several of the candles were still flickering, though most had melted down to nubs. He took one and held it up to the amulet he'd taken from the vault. There were a series of arcane markings around the perimeter, and five rubies surrounding a central diamond. Something about the pattern seemed familiar to him, but he couldn't put his finger on it. One thing he was sure of, however, was that wearing it wouldn't curse him. He didn't know why he was sure, but that sort of intuition had never led him wrong, and he was willing to trust it now.

He slipped it over his neck to see what would happen. He didn't feel stronger, or smarter, or more agile, and as far as he could tell he was still visible and hadn't learned how to fly. He shrugged and made ready to leave. A drawer revealed extra candles, and he lit one for his trip back downstairs. He needed to move quietly and quickly, so he left his satchel on the bed, hoping to come back for it later. While he decided to bring Stu's arrows and the bow he had found, he left Allison's mace next to his pack on the bed. If it came down to it, she could hit things with a torch just as easily. Reflecting on how new to the game she was, he revised his thought to *miss things just as easily*, then chuckled.

With one last look around the bedroom for anything useful, Chuck padded down the hallway. He took the stairs to the lower level and soon approached the door to the gallery. He put his eye to the peephole beside the door, hoping that his clock had been accurate and he was now in the kobolds' downtime. The gallery still had torchlight flooding everywhere, but the foot traffic had almost completely disappeared. Figuring *almost completely* was as good as he was going to get, he took his eye from the hole and approached the door.

He placed his candle on the ground, then bent his shoulders to the task of lifting the bar that braced it. Grunting with exertion, Chuck discovered the bar was much heavier when he was holding it up instead of the brackets. That explained why the door hadn't been breached: a sizeable ram would have been needed to break through. Wishing desperately that the amulet had granted him super strength, he heaved the bar up and over one of the brackets on the wall, easing the end down to the ground. He took a few moments to catch his breath and then heaved on the other side. The wood lifted but slipped out of his grasp and tumbled to the ground with a crash that echoed up and down the long corridor. Cursing, he ran back to the peephole to see if anyone on the other side had heard it.

He held his breath, waiting for some sign of alarm. At last he saw one of the kobolds passing through his field of vision perhaps fifty feet away, and it didn't spare even a glance at where he was hiding. Either the noise hadn't been heard, or it had been dismissed as one of the typical sounds you hear in old hillside fortresses. He let out a sigh of relief and returned to the door.

There was no locking mechanism that he could see. Presumably this door was kept open during normal times and was only meant to be closed in times of siege. What it did have, however, was a series of hand-operated dead bolts that secured it to the stone on both sides, the floor, and the ceiling. Most moved easily, though a couple had rusted into place and needed some light tapping to free them. He didn't worry about the noise; if no one had heard the beam dropping, the light rat-a-tat would be safe. At last, the door was completely unlocked and he was ready to open it. One more look through the peephole indicated that the coast was clear, and he cracked the door inward.

He expected to find a curtain hanging in front of him, but there was nothing at all blocking the view of the door from the gallery. It must have been amazingly well hidden for it to have survived this long undiscovered. He slid the door open a little more and then slipped through. When he turned to pull it closed behind him, he was surprised to see a big leather strap attached to the wood with heavy bolts at waist height. This was obviously a handle. He grabbed it and pulled the door closed, then looked around in confusion. How in the world had the kobolds not noticed it?

There was movement on the other side of the gallery, but otherwise the room was empty. He darted to the nearest pillar and squatted down to look around. To his amazement, the leather strap had disappeared. He rubbed his eyes to make sure he wasn't imagining it, but it really was gone. Well, that explained why the door hadn't been opened!

The next thing he had to do was figure out where his friends were being kept. This sort of complex almost certainly had a dungeon area, so he had to locate the path down. To make sure he could find the hidden door again, he scuffed the pillar with his boot, leaving a black streak across it. Nodding at a job well done, he silently padded along the wall. He didn't really have a plan other than to go down, and he had to start somewhere. When he reached the room's corner, he scanned the length of the wall and was pleased to find just a single archway leading out of it. Checking for any kobolds as he went, he dashed to the archway and peeked around the corner. He immediately ducked his head back at what he saw: two kobolds standing sentry at the base of a stairway. He assumed that this was the pathway back to the surface.

He retraced his steps along the wall, stopping when he got to the pillar with his scuff mark on it. The wall was blank, but after a few moments of feeling around it with his hand, he came across the strap he had used to close the door. As soon as he touched it, it popped back into view, and he could see the faint outline of the seam between the door and the wall. He smiled, then continued along the wall. After several steps he turned back and discovered that the illusion had returned. *Good stuff,* he thought. Wouldn't stand up to a serious search by a professional like him, but it obviously did the trick against less experienced investigation.

The other wall also had only a single archway, which he approached with caution. If this was the path down to the dungeons, it might also be guarded. Peeking around the corner, he was pleased to discover the stairs headed down and there were no guards. Perhaps the ones assigned were just lazy and had wandered off. With kobolds that wasn't out of the question. To satisfy a pestering curiosity, Chuck continued past the arch to see what the fourth wall held. Yet another arch, again unguarded, led to a tunnel with several branches visible from where he stood. The living chambers, he figured. He returned to the descending staircase.

The stairs spiraled downward, and the irregularly spaced torches flickered ominously against the walls. Chuck drew Jimmy's dagger and held it in front of him, though he wasn't sure just how much help it would be if he came across one of the kobolds. Even if he were able to dispatch one, it would almost certainly raise the alarm, and experience indicated that even the party couldn't defeat an entire tribe's worth at once. He thought back to TJ's James Bond story and shrugged. Either it would work or it wouldn't. No one could say he didn't give it his best.

At the bottom of the stairs was a single door, presumably locked. Sitting in a chair in front of the door was a kobold, his chin resting peacefully on his chest as he snored. A ring of keys dangled from the sleeping guard's belt. Chuck shook his head at his stupid luck and considered the options: He could try to kill the guard with his knife, but that could be messy and noisy, two things he didn't want in case another happened to come down the stairs. Unfortunately, he had left his poisons in the bag upstairs, in retrospect a horrible decision. Going back wasn't an option—who knew when the guards might be changed, or when this one would wake up.

He quickly made up his mind, and stepped carefully toward the guard. A brief inspection of the door revealed that it was, in fact, locked, so he needed to either pick it or swipe the keys. Years of picking pockets on the streets of Westmarch made the decision an easy one. A light swipe with a dagger separated the thong that connected the key ring to the guard's belt. With keys in hand, Chuck quickly unlatched the door, slipped through, and closed it behind him. If the guard woke up, nothing would immediately seem amiss.

As he had hoped, it was, in fact, the prison. A long line of wooden doors stretched down either side of the corridor, each with a barred window to observe the prisoners. There was just a single torch to his side, leaving the farthest cells in gloomy near darkness. It felt damp, as befitted a dungeon, though that might have just been his imagination. After closing his eyes for a few moments to improve his dark vision, he left the torch burning by the door and moved down the row of cells, peeking between the bars for signs of his friends. The first several on either side were empty, but when he reached the fourth one, he was glad that he had left the torch behind and was moving quietly. The cell was inhabited by a kobold. Chuck reflected that it was possible the prisoner was some dual-scimitar-wielding kobold ranger who had forsaken his family and his heritage. More likely it was some rabble-rouser who had irritated the chief and been thrown down here instead of getting skewered. That sort of prisoner would see him not as an opportunity for escape but as an opportunity to get himself back in his boss's good graces. Chuck continued down the hall.

The very last two cells held his friends. The one on the left had Stu, Jimmy, and Allison in it, and TJ was across the hall by himself. He nodded at the arrangement. TJ, a spellcaster, would be bound with his hands behind his back and with a gag in his mouth to keep him from using magic to escape. There was no reason why the archer and the swordsman shouldn't be together, particularly if the bars were as strong as their dwarven heritage suggested. The kobolds wouldn't have known that Allison had her own magical powers, since she didn't exhibit them during the fight. He hoped she had been able to heal the boys from the vicious wounds they received during the skirmish. The fact that Stu was alive at all—let alone conscious—after the beating he took suggested that she had. The key ring only had two keys on it, one for the door to the outside and hopefully one to open all the cell doors. He put the key in the lock to the threesome's cell and turned, pleased that it remained silent. Before he opened the door, he called out softly, "Psst." The last thing he wanted was to be ambushed by Jimmy's fists.

Not receiving an answer, he repeated louder: *"Psst!"* Still nothing. Frustrated, he called out softly, "Hey, Jimmy. It's me!"

Silence.

Shaking his head, Chuck opened the door and stuck his head in. "Hello? Are you guys paying attention? C'mon, I'm trying to rescue you!"

Three figures jumped to their feet in alarm, and the largest one moved protectively in front of the other two, fists clenched. "Who's there? Aren't you a little short to be a kobold?"

"Geez. It's me, Jimmy."

"C'mon. Come get some if you want it." Jimmy didn't sound very sure of himself.

"Hello? Am I just talking to myself right now?" Chuck crept farther into the cell so they could see he was the one who had opened the door, but he immediately had to dodge backward to avoid the fist swung at his head. The blow was clumsy, as if Allison's healing hadn't been sufficient to get him back up to fighting snuff, and he easily avoided it. Chuck stepped forward to use the larger man's inertia to trip him, and Jimmy landed face-first with a grunt. Stu and Allison were clearly still feeling the effects of the beating they had taken and were simply cowering in the back.

Chuck took two more steps forward, and Allison gave a little gasp of surprise and said, “Chuck! Is that you? Why don’t you say anything?”

“I *did*!”

A sudden flash of memory hit him, and he grinned sheepishly. He lifted the medallion up over his head and tucked it in his belt. “Can you hear me now?”

Allison threw her arms around him with a cry.

CHAPTER 21

"You've been following us the whole time? We thought you'd ditched us," Stu commented drily.

"Well, the thought certainly crossed my mind, but I guess I'm a better team player than we all thought." He added with a wink and a grin, "Who knew, huh?"

After he had established his identity, Chuck handed Stu the new bow and returned Jimmy's dagger to him. Jimmy looked at it questioningly, but as soon as the hilt was in his hand, the blade extended to become the giant two-handed sword he was used to.

"Wow! I didn't know it could do that!" He squinted at it a moment and the blade shrank down to a wide sword about two feet long. "Look! A gladius! I'm all Roman!"

"Yeah, well, let's not get too excited. I still have to get you all out of here. And keep your voices down. I don't think this amulet will mask all of our sounds, only whoever's wearing it."

Chuck's smile belied his pessimistic statement. It looked like the rescue might work out after all.

Chuck crossed the hall to unlock TJ's cell, calling out to him softly to make sure he knew he was being rescued. As he had expected, the mage's arms were shackled behind him and his mouth was gagged. He pulled the rag out of TJ's mouth, and his friend took a couple deep breaths, working his jaw open and closed a few times. Neither key worked in the shackles, but the lock was simple enough that Chuck picked it in seconds. The two rejoined the others in their cell.

Chuck gave them a brief description of how he'd gotten to this point, leaving out details that he didn't think necessary, like that whole poison dart thing. Certain secrets were secrets for a reason. "How are you guys feeling? Do you have any fight left in you, or do we need to do the dodging thing?"

Allison was the first to speak. "I'm out of magic. I used all the healing ability I had keeping these two guys from bleeding out on us. Luckily, TJ didn't take as bad a beating, because I wasn't able to get my hands on him at all. Physically, though, other than a headache, I'm not feeling so bad. I could go a few rounds if I had to."

Chuck nodded and looked at TJ, who said, "I've still got quite a few spells left, actually, but I lost my reagent pouch somewhere along the way, so I can't cast most of them. None of the materials are particularly rare, and I should be able to restock quickly once we get out of here, but in the meantime a lot of my magic will fizzle." He paused for a moment, looking thoughtful. "But considering how useless the fireballs were against these guys in the forest, that's not really a huge loss. What I do have are some magic missiles, though, and those seemed to work pretty well the first time. Until we got overwhelmed, of course."

Stu had been testing the draw of the bow Chuck had brought him. "I can draw this, no trouble. I'm pretty sure I broke a couple ribs back there, but Allison fixed them for me a few minutes ago—they're still a little tender, but I'm good."

Jimmy grunted agreement. "Yeah, I could fight if I had to. In fact, I'd kinda like it, if you don't mind. They caught us by surprise and overwhelmed us with numbers. Toe-to-toe, however, I'd be able to whoop any ten of them at once." He stated it without bravado, and everyone believed him.

Chuck looked again to TJ, who had been the de facto leader until they'd gotten captured.

TJ looked back at him and said, "Hey, you know the way out. I'm not going to get in your way."

The rogue heaved a sigh of resignation. He shrugged and motioned them back down the hallway. He could always turn the reins back over to the wizard once they got out of here.

About halfway down the hallway, they heard a small voice call out: "Wait. Take me with you." The five pulled up short, and Stu quickly drew an arrow back to his cheek. Cautiously, Chuck approached the door from which the voice had come, careful to leave the archer a line of sight in case he had to fire. He looked through the bars of the door and saw a small humanoid shape standing in the middle of the cell.

"Who are you?" Chuck whispered.

"Eggelbert, I am, of the Stone Mountain goblins. Captured I was. Eat me they will. Please take me with you? Slow you down I won't. I promise. Get out of here I want. Yes?"

Chuck looked back to his friends in the dim light. If it were up to him, he knew what the choice would be. Turn around, never look back, and forget all about the little goblin in the cage. But the looks on their faces said he was going to be overruled on this one. Though he didn't know Stu particularly well, he knew that the other three were much less mercenary in outlook than he was. Further, they had just been guests of the dungeons themselves, so they were more likely to feel camaraderie with the creature.

"OK. Give me a second." He fiddled with the key in the lock and unbolted the door, wincing at the slight grinding noise. He had gotten used to the amulet concealing sounds, and that complacency would get him dead. None of the others seemed concerned about the noise, but he knew all too well how the smallest slipup could ruin a job. He cracked the door open to reveal the diminutive figure of Eggelbert. Chuck leaned in and said loud enough for just the goblin to hear, "If you betray us, I will make you regret being born."

The prisoner swallowed loudly and gave a nod. "Believe you I do." Chuck opened the door the rest of the way, allowing the goblin to come out. He then motioned for everyone to follow him back toward the sleeping guard.

He put his fingers to his lips and pointed at the cell that held the kobold. The six crouched down to pass beneath the bars on the door, and they reached the exit without incident. Before opening the door, Chuck slipped the amulet over his head. TJ raised an eyebrow but held his tongue. Chuck peeked through the door, and the string of curses that came out of his mouth made him glad he had put the amulet back on. The chair where the guard had been snoozing was empty.

"What I wouldn't give for a sewer chute right now," he mumbled. He turned, taking the amulet back off, and said, "Well, Jimmy, I think you might get your wish. We're gonna have company waiting for us when we go up the stairs. Everyone get ready."

Jimmy held his sword out in front of him, and Stu nocked an arrow. Allison, weaponless, took the torch from its sconce and snuffed it under her boot. It wasn't as good as her mace, but it was much better than her bare hands. TJ nodded wearily and reached toward his belt, forgetting his pouch had gone missing. He let out a sigh and shrugged. No one noticed the look of determination in Eggelbert's eyes.

Chuck said, "OK, let's take it slowly. Maybe we'll be lucky and he just went to find the bathroom. Do kobolds even use bathrooms?" His question was met with blank stares, and they crept up the stairs.

Chuck peeked his head around the last bend with the rest of the group close behind. Stu crouched directly behind him, an arrow drawn. Jimmy, rather than playing rear guard the way he had done during their march, came next so that he could move in front of whom he referred to as the "squishier" members of the group. TJ, Allison, and the goblin were last. Chuck was concerned that the goblin didn't have anyone keeping an eye on him, but that was the least of their worries at this point.

He let out a sigh of relief as tension flooded out of his body. There was no welcoming party waiting for them to emerge from the tunnel. Maybe it would end up being as easy as he'd hoped. He put his hand up to tell the others to stay put and crept forward inch by inch, slowly expanding his view of the main hall. He got just to the edge of the torchlight leaking in and still didn't see anything. He motioned his friends forward, then pointed to the left.

Out into the gallery and along the wall they went, moving as quickly as they could while remaining silent. Soft noises came from the direction of the living quarters, and Chuck wondered whether he had really timed his sleep properly. They wouldn't know until they finally got out. *If* they got out. They reached the corner without incident, and Chuck's sharp eyes barely made out the mark he had left on the pillar. A cough brought him up short, and the others skidded to a halt behind him.

From behind the nearest pillar a kobold's head peeked out, a feral grin on its face and saliva dripping from its mouth. Almost immediately an arrow flew from Stu's bow, impaling the creature's forehead and dropping it to the ground. The six exchanged relieved glances, but their elation disappeared as more of the creatures piled into view. It appeared that the prison guard had gone for reinforcements.

The kobolds had wisely lured the prisoners and would-be rescuer from the cul-de-sac of the prison wing and into the open space of the great hall. The friends were now trapped in the corner with no real cover. Neither running nor hiding was an option. Even if they got to the secret door in time to get it open—and that in itself was unlikely—the kobolds would be able to break it down quickly. There would be no escape. The companions' only chance was to fight and kill enough of the kobolds to let them go rather than suffer more losses. Luckily, kobolds had never gotten the hang of archery, so the friends wouldn't have to worry about dodging arrows.

Chuck thought back to the fight at the campsite and tried to see the positive in their current situation. Despite Jimmy's claims to the contrary, the fight in the woods was pretty lopsided—it hadn't taken long for them to be overwhelmed. But they had several advantages this time around. First, they weren't surrounded. While being trapped in the corner meant there was nowhere to run, it also meant that their foes could only come from one direction. Second, they were fully awake and alert. Their bodies may not have been at the top of their game, but at least everyone was standing and ready. That said, he was all too aware of the huge disadvantage to him personally. There was no tree for him to climb for cover.

Allison was determined to take her newly acquired role of battle medic seriously. She gave TJ a pointed look and stood in front of him, ready to do better than last time. He smiled and nodded. "I'll just shoot from behind you. No more stupid dagger tricks for me."

The first wave of kobolds stormed forward, egged on by those behind. Stu drew and fired as rapidly as he could, and with each arrow one of the beasts crumpled to the ground. Howls of pain and rage echoed across the gallery. The ones that managed to cross the distance were met head-on by Jimmy and his spinning sword, which had once again become an enormous blade. His extended reach gave him a tremendous advantage, and the first several didn't even get a chance to swing their big clubs before the blade flashed across their torsos, cutting them open and sending them to their knees.

A second rank came into view, wielding wickedly curved swords rather than clubs and carrying shields with which they could defend against ranged attacks. The kobolds weren't quick enough with the shields to block Stu's arrows, but they caused him to spend more time aiming between each shot, and this meant more enemies were able to engage Jimmy. Three bore down on him at once, shields at the ready and swords flashing through the air. A blade aimed at his head was easily deflected by his sword, but that left the bottom half of him exposed, and the other two lunged with their weapons, hoping to skewer him. Somehow he was able to get his enormous sword back around to parry, but the blades still drew blood along the side of his abdomen. He grimaced in pain.

The kobold who had aimed high renewed its attack, swinging down at his head with both hands. Jimmy retreated a step and managed to block the blow, but the other two lunged again, pushing him back another step. For all his boasting, his body didn't seem to be entirely recovered from the beating he'd taken. His reflexes were just a little bit off, and his sword felt heavier than usual.

"This would be a good time for some help!" he called out, stepping back once more.

Stu continued to fire his arrows, but the three kobolds around Jimmy dodged in and out, giving him no clear targets. He could pick off only the ones that peeked their heads out from behind pillars or tried sneaking along the walls to flank them. Eventually, the kobolds learned that they were sitting ducks when advancing. Finally, they gave up trying, and he was left with no further targets.

TJ had been trying to conserve his spells as long as his fighter friend continued to hold his own. Now that things started to turn against the big man, he flung his hands out, sending bolts of energy toward the kobolds. Magically guided, they streaked past Jimmy and scored direct hits in the middle of his attackers' chests. None dropped, but they all staggered back slightly, allowing Jimmy to regain his footing and lash out. The three had clearly fought together extensively, because while the one Jimmy targeted appeared dazed and unable to parry, the other two swung their blades in tandem, deflecting his heavy sword from scoring. Jimmy grunted in frustration and took a wild swing at one of the two who had parried, but his target was prepared and easily stepped out of the way, the blade passing harmlessly in front of it.

The one on his left suddenly cried out and dropped to a knee as his leg buckled beneath him, a dagger buried to the hilt. A blur of motion turned into a second dagger that lodged itself into his elbow, and the kobold's fingers spasmed, causing it to drop its sword. Seeing an opportunity, Jimmy slashed forward, taking the creature's sword arm off completely. It toppled to the floor.

With one of their comrades down, the remaining two looked anxious about their chances, and Jimmy's face broke into a broad grin. He lashed out high at one and low at the other, and then repeated the pattern in the opposite direction. Each of his blows were deflected by the kobolds' swords, but each block was slightly slower than the one before. Both Jimmy and his quarry knew it was only a matter of time before his blade landed true. He went through the high-low pattern one more time, but rather than repeating it again on the way back, he swept his sword across the two, from low to high. The kobolds, expecting the opposite, had their shields out of position, and his blade slid across both of them without resistance. They fell in a heap atop their dead comrade.

A lull had come over the room. Stu had nearly run out of arrows and became selective in his shots, firing only when he knew he could hit. The kobolds had backed off, though the friends knew there were still plenty more. Chuck casually walked forward to where the dead kobolds lay and retrieved the two throwing daggers. He wiped them off on a kobold's fur, his nose wrinkling at the stench, then replaced them in sheaths hidden inside his sleeves.

Grinning, the small man tittered. "Good thing they didn't have a cave troll. Might I suggest this be the time to start moving again?" Chuck made an "after you" gesture toward the hidden door.

A voice boomed out. "No, I don't believe it is!" A shape stepped out from behind one of the pillars. A very big shape. The very big shape of an ogre in plate armor from neck to boots. The ogre carried a shield the size of a wagon wheel in one hand and a sword half as long as Jimmy's in the other. It shot them a feral grin and drawled, "I don't believe it is."

CHAPTER 22

"What . . . the . . . ?" was all Chuck could stutter as they looked up in horror.

"Their chief, that is," came a small voice from behind, and everyone but Jimmy turned to look for the source. It was the goblin they had rescued, whom everyone had forgotten as soon as the fighting started.

TJ rolled his eyes at the diminutive creature. "You couldn't have mentioned him earlier?" He took a couple steps forward and announced in a commanding voice, "I am Galphalon the wizard, and I seek peaceful passage for our fellowship. We have already shown our prowess in battle. Do you want to suffer the same fate as your minions?" He tried to raise himself to his full height, but his back was still stiff from the ordeal of the last several days.

The ogre let out a deep belly laugh and said, "Well *I* am Crackrock the ogre, and I don't see any reason to give you passage, peaceful or otherwise. You trespassed on my lands; you are aiding my enemies." He looked pointedly at the goblin, then gestured to the bodies lying on the ground before them. "And you've made an awful mess of my fortress, not to mention the corpses outside. I'm guessing that was your doing as well. It seems to me that if I'm to do anything, it should be to kill you and eat you."

Affronted, TJ replied, "Trespass on your lands? Your forces ambushed us a two days' march from here. How can you claim that land to be your own? Surely it belongs to someone else."

"*Belonged* to someone else, you mean." The ogre chuckled. "My master comes. Soon all of the land between the Golden Hills and the Shadowed Forest will be mine, and I will rule it with fire and steel. Those who defy me will be eliminated!" He let out a roar, which echoed back in approval from the kobolds still alive. "I had planned on discussing . . . options . . . with you, but then I heard you had released that little goblin. Now I think I will just crush you all and squeeze your marrow for my toast." A loud cheer went up at this last statement, and he stepped forward to engage the heroes.

In a bid for more time, TJ shouted, "Stop! Who is your master? Maybe we could work out that deal? How do you know he doesn't want extra help?"

The ogre cocked his head like a dog hearing a new command for the first time. "Work out a deal? How do I know that I can trust you? You are aiding my enemy, and the enemy of my master."

"We didn't know the little goblin was your master's enemy. We just brought him along out of charity—you can have him back if you want."

Allison and Chuck, as if on cue, each moved to grasp one of Eggelbert's arms.

The small voice said, "Oh, please don't give me back to him. I don't want to get eaten!"

"Shh. Let him work," hissed Allison, and gave him a wink.

"My lord is Magnus, the wizard from the East. He has emerged victorious from the civil wars of the Arcanum and now moves westward. He has promised me these lands for my own if I aid him in his conquest."

The friends briefly exchanged glances. They hadn't heard the name before, but there was little doubt that this Magnus was the guy that they were supposed to go and defeat. That he was recruiting local warlords to extend his reach was bad news. Their quest was no longer a simple trek east for a single battle. They would need to fight or sneak their way across the continent before confronting him. The one bit of good news was that it meant he didn't feel powerful enough to capture, and hold, the lands on his own.

"Magnus! But of course. Who else could it be? We have heard of this wizard, and have been traveling east to meet him." Technically true. "I think if we ended up battling, he would be very displeased by the outcome." Also technically true, assuming they were able to win.

Either TJ had said the wrong thing or the ogre had run out of patience. "Grah! Crackrock needs no help, and Crackrock will share his lands and his spoils with no one. Get ready to die, puny things. My toast is waiting!"

The giant creature stepped forward and swung his sword like a scythe, intending to mow down all of them at once. Jimmy stepped out to meet the blade with his own, and when the two collided, a mighty clang resounded throughout the chamber. While Jimmy had been able to deflect the strike, the force of the blow staggered him. His arms felt like they had been run over by a truck. He hoped there weren't many more of those in the ogre's arsenal.

The ogre readied another swing, but Stu released an arrow. Crackrock lifted his massive shield in front of him. A second arrow made it past the shield to pierce the seam of the ogre's shoulder armor, but Crackrock only laughed as he plucked the barb out and casually snapped it in half. Stu reached for another arrow, but found his quiver empty. He slung the bow back over his shoulder, snatched a sword from one of the fallen kobolds, and stepped forward next to Jimmy.

TJ unleashed another series of magical blasts, all targeting their single foe. The balls of energy exploded in rainbows of color as they landed, and both Jimmy and Stu felt ripples of energy reflected back at them from the impact. Although the ogre winced as each one hit, he seemed to shrug off the pain after a moment or two, which wasn't enough time to give Jimmy an opportunity to strike. Had TJ had his reagent pouch, he could have fired off several of the exploding balls of fire, but without it he seemed able to do nothing but irritate the ogre. He drew his dagger resignedly and prepared to fight.

Chuck was at a loss. Every instinct told him to disappear in the chaos of the battle. Certainly no one was expecting him to go through the secret door in the wall, so even if the kobolds saw him scamper away, they probably wouldn't pay much attention to him. On the other hand, he had come this far already, and it was conceivable that they could still end up being victorious. It would take something approaching a miracle, but it could happen. While he deliberated, he threw his daggers, hoping to get lucky. Both daggers flew true, sliding into seams in the ogre's bulky armor, but like the arrow that Stu had landed, they seemed to do little or no damage to the hulking brute.

Allison, for her part, had had something of a brainstorm. Looking down at the ring on her finger, she remembered the special abilities that were granted to the wearer, particularly the one about damage mitigation. It had saved her life once when it deflected the arrow. Maybe it would save her life again. At the very least, she figured it was worth a try. They were all more than likely going to die anyway, so worst-case scenario, she'd only be expediting the process. Or maybe that was best case. She had no idea what fate awaited them if they were recaptured, but it was almost certainly going to be unpleasant. Raising the torch over her head, she let out a yelp and leapt toward Crackrock.

TJ shouted "No!" as she closed in on the giant, who looked mildly amused at both her battle cry and her attack. Crackrock flicked his sword in her direction almost casually, lining it up for her to impale herself on it as she charged. To his surprise (and her relief), the blade scraped across the side of her breastplate, letting her slip behind his guard. She brought the torch crashing down into him, and a loud dull clang reverberated throughout the room. The ogre retreated a step under the force of the blow but was only stunned for a moment. He lashed out with his shield, bashing her shoulder and sending her flying headfirst into the wall. She collapsed to the ground and lay unmoving.

Crackrock laughed and called out, "Neeeext?"

Stu and Jimmy circled in opposite directions, hoping to establish some sort of flanking maneuver, but it was clear to TJ that the effort was futile. The ogre's long reach and the protection afforded by both his armor and his shield meant that this would be the end of the road. Once the ogre realized that Stu was only proficient enough with the sword to not chop his own legs off, he would focus on Jimmy and pound him into submission. With no other ideas, TJ stepped forward between the other two boys. Maybe if he was able to distract Crackrock for a moment it would give Jimmy an opportunity to strike a solid blow.

As he stood in front of the giant ogre, waiting to be chopped in half, TJ heard mumbled words from behind. It was as if they were floating through his consciousness without ever really settling in his mind. Suddenly, the hair on his head stood straight up as a bolt of energy passed over his left shoulder and hit the ogre chief directly in the chest. A spot in the middle of Crackrock's breastplate turned bright red with heat, and the color expanded outward through the rest of his armor. The ogre roared in anguish and flailed about angrily, nearly hitting TJ with his sword. The armor continued to heat up, and then suddenly, a violent light flared, causing everyone to shield their eyes. When the light dimmed and everyone could look again, all that remained of the giant and his massive armor was a small smoldering pile of ash.

"Well, that takes care of that, does it not?" The goblin giggled and then turned to Chuck. "Your escape plan. Pursue it we should, no?"

Chuck nodded, and once Jimmy heaved Allison over his shoulder, he led them along the wall and through the secret door. Not wanting to take any chances, Chuck took the time to slide the dead bolts, securing the door back into the stonework. With Jimmy's help, Stu put the bar back across it as well, guaranteeing them plenty of time to make good their escape. The extra effort was unnecessary, however. If any of the kobolds were interested in avenging their leader's death, they exhibited it only by fleeing from the show of power that had just vaporized him.

CHAPTER 23

Not long after that, the six were walking in the woods several miles from the kobolds' lair. Eggelbert had offered them the hospitality of his clan as a show of gratitude for rescuing him, and they eagerly accepted. They marched slowly because Jimmy still had to half carry Allison. She was lucky that she'd suffered only a few broken ribs, and likely a concussion. The way she had fallen in a heap when she crashed made TJ worry she'd broken her neck, but it seemed that even low-ranked heroes were made of pretty stern stuff.

Despite their slow pace, there had been no sign of pursuit. In fact, there hadn't even been any sign of the guards outside the tunnel entrance when they emerged from the secret exit. Eggelbert surmised that with the power vacuum created by Crackrock's death, the only thing the kobolds cared about for the time being was who would get to be the new chief. The biggest and toughest would duke it out head-to-head as the more subtle of them plotted assassinations.

"They have subtle ones?" TJ asked in disbelief.

"Indeed, yes, they do. Rarely seen they are, and rarely expose themselves. They know that kobold society is not built around smarts, but strength. So they seek to blend in as best they can. Yes? And fear the smart ones, the dumb ones do, so the ones that don't blend in get, how do you say, eliminated? Yes? While young they still are. Did you not wonder why no bows they used, but instead charged in to be given the old chop-chop by your friend?" He jerked a thumb at Jimmy. "Not tough enough are bows. Only clubs and rarely swords."

TJ nodded. "I guess that makes sense. But how do you know they exist at all, if they try so hard to blend in?"

The goblin simply shrugged. "Exist they do."

At nightfall, the group stopped and made camp. It wasn't particularly comfortable since they didn't have their bedrolls, and the only food was from what Chuck had squirrelled away before he set off to rescue them. Stu had found some arrows in the dwarven royal chambers and offered to go hunt, but his offer was halfhearted and everyone knew it. They told him to just try to recuperate by the fire. Everyone had bumps and bruises, and while the gash that Jimmy took had been bandaged with dwarven sheets, it still hurt enough to make him not want to move more than necessary.

The group sat around the fire in silence, chewing on the dried meat Chuck had passed around. After a time spent studying the goblin closely, TJ finally asked the question that was on everyone's mind. "So, um, how did you do that to the ogre back there? And if you could do that, how'd you get yourself captured in the first place?"

Eggelbert giggled and replied, "Patient you were, to wait so long to ask. I bet of goblins you think the same as kobolds, yes? None too bright, yes? Surprised you would be at what you know not about the others who live in this world.

"A wizard I am," he continued. "Rare, it is true. But mighty and powerful I am. Three hundred years we goblins live, did you know? Only ninety years live even the oldest humans. Much time to study have I. And much time to learn. And much time to perfect. Lived one hundred eighty years I have, and study and learn I still do. Perhaps I learn not as quickly as you, but learn more I can. And have." He nodded.

"As for how I got captured, well, how did you get captured, hmm? Four bodyguards you had, and still got captured you did, mighty wizard." He shrugged. "Happens it does. And while disintegrate any of my jailers I could have done, only one it would have been, and many they were. That spell—I meant to use on their leader." He leaned closer and shared a conspiratorial look. "Captured I meant to be. But to get locked in the jail I did not. Meet the chief I was to do. And kill the chief I was to do."

Chuck grinned. "So you were sent to assassinate him?"

The goblin shrugged. "Bad the ogre was, and being attacked was my tribe. What I needed to do, I did."

"Which tribe, did you say?" Allison suddenly asked.

The goblin's eyes glinted with mirth. "Stone Mountain I said, though of Stone Mountain I am not. Being clever I was. And sneaky. Now that I know friends you are, tell the truth I shall. Bonecrusher clan I am." He puffed out his chest and sat up a little straighter.

Allison gave a laugh. "Bonecrusher! Of course you are. We were told about you when we first started our quest. Another goblin told us that you were facing a great danger. He implied that we were supposed to help somehow. Was this that great danger?"

Eggelbert nodded his head enthusiastically. "Indeed. No greater danger has the Bonecrusher clan ever met. Captured much of our lands Crackrock has, with the help of his evil master, and many of our finest he killed." He looked sad, and Allison wondered whether he had suffered some personal loss as well. "The last hope of my tribe I was. If unsuccessful I was, then all hope would be lost, and become no more would the Bonecrusher tribe. But as the sun rises and sets, so too did his evil plans. And while defeated the evil wizard is not, slowed he will be, and set back will be his plans." He broke out into a grin. "But helped us you did. And for that, grateful we will be!"

In a deadpan voice Chuck said, "I seem to recall there was some mention about shinies . . . ?"

Allison shot him a dirty look, but Eggelbert exclaimed, "Oh yes! Many shinies have we, and many shinies shall you have too!" The goblin continued to giggle, though what he found funny no one was entirely sure.

Just then a loud cawing noise came out from the darkness, and a bird swooped down toward the campsite. Stu had an arrow nocked in his bow and was ready to fire when Eggelbert said, "No!" Reluctantly, Stu lowered his bow, and the friends watched in amazement as the bird landed right on the goblin's head.

"That's not . . . ," Chuck began, and trailed off.

"Yup! My familiar this is! Led you to me he did, no? A good birdie my Pogo is!" He offered the bird a morsel of the dried meat, but it shook its beak at him and flew back into the trees. "Good taste he has too!"

Silence descended over the camp as each retreated to their own thoughts. After a time, Chuck said, "You guys go ahead and sleep. I slept on a bed fit for a king last night. I can take the first watch tonight." There was no chance anyone was going to rely on magical wards or simple bell traps to protect them after the last time they settled in by the campfire. At the looks he received from the others, he added, "And I won't go up into the tree until after it's my watch. I promise. Though you can't argue with the outcome, can you?"

He received mostly blank looks before they all rolled over to get some sleep, though Jimmy flashed a wry grin in appreciation of his joke.

The goblin raised an eyebrow at the odd exchange and then shrugged. "Sleep I will too. Watch I can take as well. Wake me."

Chuck shook his head. "Nah, I got this. Enjoy your first night out of the clink. I slept on feathers last night."

As snores began to rise from his companions one by one, Chuck sat and thought about the shinies the goblins had assured them they would receive. Patting the pouch of gemstones tucked inside his satchel, he thought that even if the promised reward turned out to be nothing more than mere trinkets, he'd be coming out of the deal pretty far ahead. Pretty far ahead indeed.

CHAPTER 24

The group rose with the sun the next morning, battered and bruised but optimistic for the first time since before Simon had been killed. Chuck had let them sleep through the night, and while he was a little groggy, it made a huge difference in everyone else's outlook. They were eager to get a move on, so breakfast was short. They marched in silence until Stu, still limping, spoke.

"I owe you an apology, Chuck. I thought the worst of you, and I was wrong." He lapsed back into silence.

After a time, the thief responded. "Nah, don't sweat it. You had every right to think as you did. I sure would have if I were you." His brow furrowed. "I'm not going to lie; it was a tough call. Part of me—I think the same part that made me hide before—kept trying to convince me to forget you and go make a life for myself. I'm glad I didn't follow his advice."

"Not nearly as much as we are," Allison said, smiling.

"I know exactly what you mean, little guy," replied Jimmy. "Back at the bandit camp I thought I was just caught up in the newness of everything. But back in the cell it was like there was another person trying to bust out of me. And bust some heads. As much as I like to be the big man who keeps an eye on everyone else, I'm not too sure I'm so happy about this change."

"Well, from my perspective, it's pretty sweet." All heads turned toward TJ. "I mean, let's face it, Galphalon is me, just more so. Bookish, not terribly athletic . . . I've even gained phenomenal cosmic powers, like a djinn, but without the downside of the itty-bitty living space à la Disney's *Aladdin.* All the knowledge rolling around in my head right now? Not a bad deal, if you ask me." Seeing the looks of surprise on his friends faces, he added, "Not that I want to stay here, of course. But it could be a lot worse."

Eggelbert looked confused but held his tongue.

"Well, I don't really feel any different," said Allison as she trudged along. "Still just little old me. And I definitely don't want to stay here."

It took two more days of traveling to get to the goblins' home. While Allison's healing ability was great for closing wounds or mending broken bones, it didn't help with aches and pains, much to everyone's disappointment. They continued to limp along for most of the journey. It wasn't until they had gotten all the way to Eggelbert's town that everyone felt back to normal.

After a time, their path crossed a dirt road with wagon ruts worn into it, and they gratefully turned to follow this easier terrain. Allison reflected that it hadn't been so long ago that their journey had started in much the same manner. As they rounded a bend in the road, the forest around them abruptly fell away, and a wooden palisade came into view at the base of some low mountains. Each of the logs that made up the wall was sharpened into a spike, and thin pennants flew at towers at regular intervals.

At this point Eggelbert stepped forward and said, "First I should be now, so known to my tribe we will be."

When they got closer, it became clear that the logs in the palisade were actually fifty-foot tree trunks, and the pennants they had spied from afar were enormous banners.

"Wow," TJ managed to say at the sight. Despite being constructed only of wood, the fortress was an architectural marvel.

"Someone built this with siege in mind," added Jimmy with a nod. A span of a hundred yards had been clear-cut between the woods and the walls, giving the goblins a good field of vision for the catapults almost certainly hidden behind the walls. The cleared area had been planted with corn, which was ready to be harvested. Movement between the spikes indicated that there was a platform running along the top that would allow archers to fire from behind cover. "Given their neighbors, can't say that I'm surprised."

"Indeed, to survive, adapt we must, my people have found. The days of huts and caves and peace—gone they are. Instead, to the Bonecrushers, war and strife have come. From kobolds has it come. And from humans. From many. So adapt we have." Eggelbert sounded resigned. Being almost two hundred years old, he could probably remember better times.

"So tell me," Allison said as they approached the gate. "Why are you called the Bonecrushers? That doesn't sound particularly peaceful. Sounds to me like we've got as much to fear from you as you do from us."

Eggelbert giggled. "The Bonecrushers we are because soup we like, and the best soup stock from crushed bones comes, yes?" With a twinkle in his eye, he continued. "A good name for times like these it is too. No?"

Allison chuckled along with the rest of the group. "A very good name for times like these, I agree!"

A sentry upon the wall called out a challenge in the goblin's vowel-heavy language, but when he saw Eggelbert was in the lead, the tone of his voice changed. The guard turned and shouted toward the interior of the palisade, waving his arms in excitement. After a few moments, the heavy wooden gate was raised from the inside.

As they passed through the portal, the goblin said, "As friends you come. Promise not to spy you must. Yes?"

Everyone nodded.

Once they were inside the palisade walls, the gate slowly closed, groaning as the ropes passed through a series of pulleys. The goblins had dug holes along the bottom and reinforced them with stone so that the logs acted like a portcullis on a human castle. Turning around, they could see a series of reinforcing beams that could be placed across the gate in case a ram was used against it. In all, it looked to be a solid structure.

Behind the wall was a town of considerable size. The streets were not cobbled, and the buildings were no more than a single story, but otherwise it looked very much like a human settlement. Businesses and craftsmen had signs hanging above their doorways advertising their wares. Laughing children chased chickens, never quite catching their elusive prey. Parents kept a watchful eye on their children as they went about their business—sweeping, or baking, or working at the forge.

"My home this is. Welcome you are," Eggelbert said with a flourish.

Some of the guards seemed to know their guide, if not his mission, and they looked expectantly toward him for some sign. When he returned their inquisitive looks with a toothy grin and a nod, relief spread across their faces and they broke out into grins of their own. The information traveled quickly, and while children were shooed behind skirts at the sight of the humans, there were many happy faces looking toward Eggelbert as he walked down the street. He good-naturedly returned smiles to all he saw.

At the base of the mountainside were Greek-like pillars flanking an exquisitely carved tunnel entrance. Across the top were depictions of what appeared to be the goblin pantheon. Along the sides were much more terrestrial goblins engaged in farming and trades, as well as other tasks that hardly looked worthy of capturing in stone.

TJ said, "I recognize the gods Tahooah and Gahrauah, and their children, but the images over there"—he gestured to the sides—"are not familiar to me. I would have expected carvings of heroes defeating dragons and the like."

At the spoken names of his gods, Eggelbert placed his hand over his heart and then lips. "Heroes of my people those *are*. The ones who first learned to craft pots and tools. The ones who learned to cultivate the land and to husband the livestock. To them the greatest debt my people owe, and so immortalized they are." He added, sort of as an afterthought, "Of course, who any of those people actually were we don't know, but beside the point that is. Within is where all his business our chief does. Well, his official business. For the other kind, the latrine he uses." This set him into another fit of the giggles.

Jimmy elbowed Stu and murmured, "Well, at least bathroom humor is universal."

Allison rolled her eyes. "So are we headed in to meet the chief?"

"Yup! The plan that is! A good chief Finkelbert is. Eager to know the details he will be. And to meet you."

The friends crossed a wide square surrounding a small bubbling fountain. There was a short line of goblins with buckets waiting their turn to collect water for their homes. As soon as each filled its bucket, the creature set off slowly trying to keep it from sloshing too much. The goblins in the line were chattering away, but a silence fell over them as the group passed by. Children openly gaped, and while the adults were too polite to stare, they watched out of the corner of their eyes with interest and excitement. Eggelbert smiled and waved and continued to lead the group toward the tunnel.

"The last time we went into a place like this, things didn't really turn out so well." Stu looked anxious, and he reached back to his quiver, stroking the feathers on one of his arrows.

Eggelbert stopped short and turned to look at the archer. "Kill you we could have, many times by now. Kill you *I* could have, many times by now." His face softened. "Completely safe you will be. My promise is yours. Yes?"

"He's right, Stu," Jimmy added. "I'm feeling pretty good right now, about as good as I've felt since we got here. There's no way I could fight off the whole pack of 'em. If they want us dead, we're dead. May as well just go along and hope things turn out OK."

Stu didn't look placated, but he took his hand off the arrow and nodded. Their goblin guide nodded back and turned to continue walking as if nothing had happened. There were no guards posted at the entrance. Eggelbert explained that no guards were needed. It was impossible for anyone inside the compound to be a danger to their chief, and anyone outside the compound would have to get through the gate and fight through town. If they could do that, another one or two guards wouldn't make a difference. They passed through the columns, upon which delicate carvings were etched.

The tunnel led to a small room with a desk and a goblin behind it. There were several piles of paper stacked on the desk, as well as a large inkwell. The goblin wrote with a large quill pen, occasionally dipping it into the well.

When the group had finished filing into the room, he looked up and said, "Ah. So you have returned, Eggelbert. And your mission? I hear it went well?" Out of politeness for his guests, the chief spoke in the human tongue rather than goblin. It appeared that he had a better grasp of the human language than most and didn't speak with the same awkward grammar, though his voice carried the same lilt typical to his race.

"Yes, Chief, very well it went indeed." He bobbed his head a couple times but then blushed. "Well, captured I was, though at first their warlord I did not see. But these humans, helped me they did. And dead Crackrock is, and in chaos his kingdom. Little we have to fear from them now."

"Little to fear from the kobolds, perhaps, but the threat of war is out there still. This was only a minor battle in the fight for Livonia."

"The fight for Livonia?" TJ asked in a surprised voice. "Why do you care about what happens to our kingdom?"

The chief gave him a severe look, but then his features softened. "Of course we care about you, my boy. Your human kingdom is what ensures peace in this area, though perhaps not the peace we would prefer." He smiled and added, "Who are the devious ones, hmm? Not the Bonecrushers, that is for sure."

"That was *you*?" TJ's jaw dropped at the thought that the goblin they'd almost killed at the beginning of the adventure was actually the tribe's chief.

At this, Eggelbert cried, "Their aid you enlisted?"

The chief put up his hands in a sign of supplication and said to TJ, "Yes, that was me. There are some jobs that need to be done and can't be trusted to others. Nor would I have asked another to risk a meeting with a band of adventurers, since you are typically more interested in what sort of loot creatures drop than anything." He looked directly at Chuck, who had the good graces to study his own shoes for a bit. Turning to the other goblin, he continued. "I could have sent you, Eggelbert, but you had your own mission. And yes, I enlisted their aid. These are extraordinary times, which call for extraordinary measures." He suddenly looked tired. "I hoped that you would be successful, but I knew that even if you were, you would probably never return to us. If you failed, then perhaps they would succeed. And if you succeeded, then perhaps they would find us and bring us word of your success. That you were successful and able to return to us is well beyond anything I had begun to hope for."

Eggelbert said coldly, "My wife, while gone I was, you married not?"

The two goblins looked at each other, and the humans shifted their weight from side to side during the awkward silence. The chief's lips twitched and then finally broke into a full laugh, which was accompanied by Eggelbert's high-pitched giggling. Allison exchanged glances with TJ, who shrugged back.

When the wizard had caught his breath, he explained, "The chief's big sister my wife is." He began to giggle again. The humans smiled at the joke.

"So what now, Chief Finkelbert?" TJ asked.

"Well, that is up to you. As I told you when we first met, you are welcome to any of our treasure. We may even have tucked away some items of power that could benefit you in the future. And you are welcome to stay here within our walls for as long as you would like. You are one of us now, in deed if not in blood. We will not turn you out. Beyond that . . ." He paused and shrugged. "Beyond that, you may do as you wish. Your king's mission still awaits you. Defeating Crackrock was only the first step in the process, and it has done nothing but buy you time. The mage from the East will still come, and come with power. Even with our success today, he will be victorious unless you take an active hand. I believe in my heart that would be a disaster for your people, not only for mine."

He paused a moment and looked at the other goblin. "Would you please excuse us for a moment, Egg? There's something your companions and I should discuss alone. Besides," he added with a smile, "there is someone eagerly waiting for you."

The wizard bobbed his head and walked out, waving to his new friends and completely unperturbed by his sudden dismissal.

When they were alone, Finkelbert continued. "And then there's your . . . predicament." At the surprised looks on their faces, he waved his hand. "Yes, yes, I know that you're not from around here. And before you ask, while I'm grateful that you are here to help, I had nothing to do with summoning you to our realm. But you're here, and you're not there. Assuming you want to go back—just sitting around isn't going to get the job done. I don't know how you got here, or why, or even how to send you back." He paused a moment. "You are going to have to find your own way. We cannot help you, nor can the king of your people, nor any of his advisers or wizards. The power you need can only be found within the Arcanum. For that, you will have to travel east. Do you understand?"

The friends exchanged anxious looks and put their heads together.

"I don't like this," murmured TJ.

"What's not to like?" replied Jimmy. "He's offering us a safe place to stay while we get things sorted out. I don't know about you, but I kinda like not sleeping in the woods."

"Well, we know he's already used us once to kill off one of his enemies," the wizard said with a grimace. "How do we know he isn't just trying to rope us into taking out another? This Magnus guy is *bad news*."

Stu nodded thoughtfully, and Allison added, "Look, whether or not he's trying to use us is beside the point right now. This is still far too new and foreign to us to go traipsing about aimlessly. I need to get used to the situation. Probably have a really good cry. This is as good a place to do that as any."

Jimmy puffed out his chest. "Well, if they try anything, I'll be ready this time. I failed to keep you safe once. I won't let it happen again."

Chuck nodded. "Me either. I'm pretty good at sniffing out trouble." With a twinkle in his eye, he added, "You all have my dagger."

Smiling back at the rogue, Stu added, "And my bow!"

In a terrible impression of Gimli from *The Fellowship of the Ring*, Allison chimed in, "And mah axe!"

The friends all burst out laughing.

TJ straightened and stepped forward to the chief, who looked on in quiet amusement. "Well, the one thing we agree on is that this isn't the time to be making any rash decisions. We will accept your kind offer of hospitality for the time being. As you said, Crackrock's death has bought us some time, and we need to recover and learn a bit more about our 'predicament.' Perhaps you would be able to assist us?"

The chief nodded. "In truth, I know little more than I have told you already. Still, I have ways to gather information, and I will put them at your disposal."

"Fair enough." TJ turned to his friends and said with a sigh, "It's shaping up to be a bit more than a weekend adventure, huh, guys?" He looked Jimmy straight in the eye with a wide smile and said, "I don't know about the rest of you, but I'm hungry!"

ACKNOWLEDGMENTS

This book would not exist without the tremendous support of my family, who gave me the freedom and peace and quiet to write. Thank you to my beta readers, Amy, Andrew, Bobbie, Danielle, John, and Marianne, who provided me with innumerable suggestions to make my writing better while still managing to convince me that this thing was worth reading. Thank you as well to the professionals at both Inkshares and Girl Friday Productions. Their expertise has been invaluable to me throughout the publication process. I can't overstate the influence of my editor, Kiele Raymond. Her insight and expertise made this book better in every imaginable way, from the writing to the character development to the pacing. I cannot wait to work with her on the sequel. Lastly, even after all that work, my copyeditor, Michael Trudeau, found so many more ways to improve the manuscript. Thank you.

During the crowdfunding and contest portion of this process, my friends and colleagues stepped up in a huge way. I am eternally grateful to each of you. Thank you to the folks at the Nerdist for sponsoring the contest. It led me to meet some really cool authors and read some great books. Special gratitude goes to my friend Marianne, at whose insistence I entered the contest in the first place. Without her egging me on, I would almost certainly not be writing these acknowledgments now. And last, thank you to Chris Baty for coming up with the crazy idea of National Novel Writing Month. Dear reader: You too have a novel just bursting to come out. Sit down and write it.

About the Author

Photo © Tony Llerena, www.tonyllerena.com

Dave Barrett lives with his wife, three children, and an active imagination in Hampden, Maine, where he teaches financial accounting at the University of Maine. *It's All Fun and Games* is the first in his series of young adult novels and was selected as a winner of the inaugural Nerdist Collection Contest.

LIST OF PATRONS

This book was made possible in part by the following grand patrons who preordered the book on inkshares.com. Thank you.

Amy Barrett
Andrew Barrett
Angela Powell
Angie M. Jacobson
Anne Bizup
Becky Mallory
Christopher Barrett
Clint Relyea
Danielle Barrett
Edward J. Yock II
Emily Howe
Eva Barrett
James N. Barrett
Jason Harkins
Jennifer Schreiber
Jessica Dickel
Jim Barrett and Family
Joe Carroll
Keri De Angelo
Kevin Dolley
Larry Wade
Laura Osbourne
Lisa Hall
Margaret Criner
Martha Broderick
Sarah Porter
Sue DeMoss
Tristan Harvie
Wanda Cota Dove

INKSHARES

Inkshares is a crowdfunded book publisher. We democratize publishing by having readers select the books we publish—we edit, design, print, distribute, and market any book that meets a preorder threshold.

Interested in making a book idea come to life? Visit inkshares.com to find new book projects or to start your own.

NERDIST

Founded by Chris Hardwick, Nerdist is a many-headed beast. With a sprawling podcast network, premium video content, and a flagship site for breaking entertainment news, Nerdist is a nexus for passionate, intelligent, and engaged community to come together and celebrate their wonderfully nerdy interests. Whether it's *Doctor Who* or the science behind Iron Man's armor, if you nerd out about it, we do too.

Listen in or join the conversation at nerdist.com.